TIME TO KILL

TIME TO KILL

TERRY SPAIN

CUTTING EDGE

ISBN-13: 978-1-962896-92-4

Published by
Cutting Edge Books
PO Box 8212
Calabasas, CA 91372
www.cuttingedgebooks.com

CHAPTER ONE

I T WAS early evening. I was gumshoeing along a lonely, dark lane in Central Jersey near the home of one Dominic Parente. One reason for my caution was that I had taken the trouble to find out a lot about Parente, and two of the things I knew were that he was a boss racketeer and that he owned a score of punks. One of the things I *didn't* know was how many of the goons he kept hanging around his place.

Suddenly I spotted a dim light in the distance. I hopped across a ditch full of stagnant water and into the protection of a copse of pine trees, and worked my way through their close ranks toward the light. The rows of trees ended abruptly and I halted. Across a short, flat expanse of well-kept back lawn I saw a massive mansion, dark but for the light spilling from an open doorway. Its roof was studded with many dormers, and three tall chimneys pierced the deep blue of the summer night.

I glanced at the luminous hands of my strapwatch and waited for five minutes. Nothing moved, and no sound came from the doorway or the darkness around it. Only that light at the doorway gave any indication that anyone was here, but to me for once a light in a doorway was not a friendly sign; it just said *don't come too near.*

Nine months ago Parente, in his late fifties and feeling expansive, I guess, had widened his very successful rackets and introduced marijuana and heroin into this county. Some months later a seventeen-year-old kid named Sherry Dalgren, like God-knows-how-many thousands of others kids, smoked a reefer. The stuff hooked her. Sherry switched to heroin, and during a fit of depressive mania, she committed suicide. That's the case against you, Dominic Parente—you killed Sherry Dalgren. There might be no story for me to tell, except that the local law feeds at your dirty trough. That's why Sherry's father hired me, Mack Barry, a private investigator from New York City. Tonight you were lucky, Parente, I was only on reconnaissance. It wasn't your time to die.

I crept to the edge of the rectangle of light on the lawn and peered inside. The light came from under the opaque shade of a large lamp resting on a narrow table against one wall. The only other thing I could see was the corner of a white rug.

Softly I circled to the other side of the patch of light, and the view improved. As the details registered, I muttered, "Ke-rist," but not very loud.

This was Parente's solarium. Banks of flowers bloomed in shiny copper tubs. Claret-colored cushions padded tubular chairs and benches. Yellow drapes, bright as the wing of a wild canary, masked the curve of windows and trailed gracefully on the white rug. The setting was costly, obvious proof that Parente's rackets had paid off, but the furnishings weren't what really caught my eye.

Deep within a fan-backed chair sat a young woman, motionless, her eyes closed. There was a dark loveliness about her face, thick lashes and brows matching the crown of black curls, blueish eye shadow contrasting dramatically with the carmine of perfectly molded lips. Her bone structure was clean and strong.

She wore a skirt of hunter green and a sleek white sweater. Her hips were narrow and her waist flat, like that of a lithe, growing boy, and her breasts, under the white sweater, were round and high and joyously proud, even in her sleep. She was young, certainly not over twenty-five. She sat carelessly, slumped down, hands dangling from the arms of the chair, one ankle across the opposite knee. Her legs were slim and lovely—rounded knees, beautiful calves tapering smoothly down to tiny ankles. She wore high-heeled red pumps, and I wondered if her toenails were lacquered red like her fingernails.

That's a hell of a lot of description for only one woman, but she was a lot of woman.

During my scrutiny, she had not moved or opened her eyes. She was asleep, a beautiful woman young enough to be Dominic Parente's daughter or old enough to be his mistress. She had a lovely, clean look, and seemed so out of place in this place that I forgot the danger and waded right in. I knocked on the door jamb.

She didn't wake up. I knocked again, harder. Her body shivered gently, the ankle that lay across her knee sliding smoothly down to lay across her other ankle. Then I did something else I shouldn't have done.

I said, "May I come in?"

"Come in."

With the invitation I was through the door and standing on the virginal rug. Her eyes were still closed, and her lips an intriguing pout. As her breathing deepened, her breasts pushed invitingly against the tight white sweater.

I blurted the first words that popped into my mind. "I'm lost on a shortcut off the turnpike and my car's stuck and I saw your light. May I use your phone?"

"Eh?"

"May I use your phone?"

"Oh."

"Your *telephone*, miss."

She was so lovely that I had missed the details of a bottle of Scotch and an upset glass within the shadow of the chair. She wasn't asleep. All by her beautiful self, this girl was drunker than a lush at four A.M. She mumbled, "Pour me a drink."

That broke the spell. I poured the glass quarter-full, set it within her fingers. With the special sort of mental radar of the very drunk, she sensed the procedure and gripped the glass. Lifting the glass, she began to drink slowly. Scotch trickled down her esophagus and I could almost hear it splash into the Scotch lake in her stomach. Presently, the empty glass slid to the rug.

It was time to telephone and shove off. My convertible had one wheel stuck in a ditch, and I needed help. Besides, my pulsing manhood has a very low boiling point in the vicinity of beautiful women.

"Miss, may I use your telephone?"

Not once had her eyes opened. Her chin lowered vaguely, which I interpreted as permission. There was no phone in the solarium, so I pushed open a solid swinging door. I slipped through and the door closed.

I was in a broad, high, shadowy hallway that ran the length of the house. I noticed a wall-to-wall rug, several closed doors, a carved chair and a table with a telephone on it. I stood in the security of deep shadows, but there was a circular lobby up ahead lighted with a ceiling globe.

There was need for hurry. I sat down, used the phone and whispered to the operator, "Midwood 3928."

A voice with a smile in it said, "Thank you."

While the phone buzzed, I thought back. The city of Midwood lay several miles east of the lane behind Parente's mansion. An army buddy of mine, Willy Pickle, lived there and ran a flower and bulb business. During the war, we had been together in the Pacific. Often we had talked together, planning ahead. It had seemed like a good idea to be partners in some small business in the country somewhere; but when the war ended, I returned to private investigation and Willy settled in Midwood, where a deceased uncle had willed him this flower business. He was a bachelor by inclination, definitely not a tomcat like myself. If Willy had an urge, he dated a woman for one night, then forgot about it, repeating the procedure with another woman in a month or so. Willy knew this county. I planned to stop with him for a few days and pick up some information.

After several rings, I heard Willy grumble, "Now who the hell's up this late?"

"Willy, don't interrupt. I've only got seconds to talk. This is Mack, understand? *Mack.* My car is stuck in a ditch—on the back road—past Dominic Parente's house. Fetch your jeep and—"

"Hey, you old son!"

"Don't interrupt again. There's no time. How soon can you bail me out?"

"You sneaked into town, you old son!"

"Did you get the message straight?"

"Sure. What's all the rush, anyway?"

"Can you come right out? It's important."

"Make it fifteen minutes, pal. The jeep's got a flat and—" Sudden pause. "Mack, where you phonin' from?"

"Off the lane."

"You're in trouble again! Parente's got the only phone on that road. You must be—"

Very quietly, I cradled the phone. Somewhere off the lobby, there was the noise of a door opening. Then the door slammed shut and two voices mingled in anger. Sweat popped out on my face. My gun was in the glove compartment of the convertible. I did the only thing possible. I crawled under the table and hunched there, shivering.

The voices unscrambled. A coarse voice scratched angrily, "I don't want no more of your crap!"

A second voice drawled, "You'll take what crap I feed you."

"You dumb flatfoot! You knocked off two of our pushers last week. You can get concrete shoes for that."

"Don't bore me. I know what I'm doing. Look, I make certain loud noises and everybody gets the idea I got the county under my badge. You can hire some more pushers."

"You want us to stop the ice?"

Two men drifted under the lobby light and stopped. The closer man was short, hatless and wide-shouldered, dressed in a business suit. The second man was tall and lean, his face hidden under the pulled-down brim of a hat.

The tall man drawled, "Cut off the ice and I'll run you all in. I come out here to gab with your boss. That's an order."

"You'll get told off!"

"Bub, here's another order. We'll down a couple of quick ones from the boss's private bottle and then we'll talk to the boss."

They moved into what must have been a continuing corridor that crossed the hallway where I crouched. Another door slammed and their voices died. It was my lucky night.

A cop and a crook had said things that were definitely not meant to be overheard. I understood specifically why Sherry Dalgren's father had got no cooperation from the local authorities. *Ice* is jargon for graft. With ice Parente had a green light to operate openly. Who was the fat cat who took the top share of the ice, and handcuffed the honest police so that Parente's rackets thrived?

I had no time for questions. If they found me here, they would bury me deep. Fortunately, they hadn't seen me. Nobody knew I was here, except the eyeless lush in the solarium. To her, I was merely a talking shadow. The idea was to slip into the solarium, stalk past the lush, skulk through the open doorway, and fade into the obscurity of the pine trees.

I crawled to my feet. That last slug of Scotch had surely killed the lush for the night.

But a joker had rewritten the script.

When I stepped into the solarium, the girl leaned around the side of the fan-backed chair. Her eyes were as black as her hair, and they were full of curiosity. She was sober now.

"Hello, there," she offered casually, and her voice had a soft, pleasant sound, like inquisitive rain at the window.

"Hello, again."

"Oh, have we met before?"

"Yes. When I came into the solarium from the lawn. You told me I might use your phone, miss."

"And?"

I crossed the rug and faced the chair. Her knees were lovely. "I had a flat tire," I lied, "and didn't want to change it. I saw your light. I tried to phone, but the wire was busy and—" I smiled down at her. "Before I went to the phone, you asked for a drink. I poured and you drank. Teach me sometime."

"To drink?"

"To drink when I'm out cold."

"I don't remember the incident." The sparkle went out of her eyes. "I suppose it's partly reflex. Plus habit. You know, the body builds a tolerance against liquor and the more you drink the less drunk you get. Does that sound logical?"

"Yes, but not for why you drink alone."

"When a person has a lot on her mind—" She broke off. "Are you local?"

Get out of here, Barry. They bury witnesses.

"I took a shortcut off the highway to visit an old acquaintance. Thanks for the hospitality."

"Won't you have a drink?"

"Not now."

"I'm Mrs. Dominic Parente. My first name is Elizabeth, but I prefer *Biz*. And you?"

"Just Vic Watts, and not very important. I'm from Camden."

"How do you do, Mr. Watts. Some Scotch?"

"I'm late."

"Darn, and you seem so interesting." Mrs. Parente leaned forward, her face animated. "I can't let you leave with that question on your face unanswered! I dare you to ask it!"

"Not *that* question."

"Please."

"Unh, unh."

"We'll make it a game. Is the question about me?"

"In a way."

"About my sweater?"

"Well—"

"Men! Believe me, Mr. Watts, there *is* something under my sweater." She glanced at a platinum wristwatch. "Goodness, it's five minutes past ten and I had a—ummm, when you were in the hallway, did you see anybody?"

"No."

"Servants?"

"No."

"They should be about. Perhaps a tall, lean man?"

"No."

"Stocky man?"

"No stocky man."

"Nobody talking?"

"No."

"What were they talking about?"

I said, "I didn't see anyone."

"Don't lie to me. I have a temper."

"I don't care how much temper you have, Mrs. Parente. I had a flat tire and—"

"I'm sorry," she interrupted. "You have a temper, too. Ummm, do you like beautiful women?"

"Yes."

"Let me read your character, Mr. Watts." She cupped a palm over her chin. "You're rather inscrutable, I think. You like women, but I think you like to be the one who does the choosing, and—"

At the other end of the solarium a bell rang sharply. Mrs. Parente stood erect in one fluid movement. One hand tightened on the table's edge until the knuckles stood out whitely, like picked bones. *There was danger in this house. Parente was in conference with the law.*

"My summons," she explained, and picking up the bottle, drank. She poised on high heels, every body line alive, the breasts challenging. She flipped the empty bottle to the rug for the houseman to pick up and asked quietly, "How tall are you?"

"Six feet."

"Weight?"

"A scant hundred eighty."

"Athletic?"

"Not particularly."

"Tough?"

"At the moment, rather weak."

Two flowing steps brought her too close. "I'm so unhappy here." Her body was a caress and she placed soft, wet lips against mine. Her hand pressed the back of my neck and forced my lips harder against hers. I forgot the danger. Lingeringly, her lips withdrew, and I was sorry. She swung across the rug, pirouetted.

"You're nice to kiss," she murmured. "Come again, darling, when I'm not so busy." For a moment, she swayed in her own alcoholic breeze. "I need a strong man. Like you!"

I tried to go to her, but my legs had the consistency of wet macaroni. Before I could make them behave like legs again, she had backed through the swinging door, smiling. She was drunk again. In this house, she had to down all the Scotch she could find to bulwark her self-respect. Or perhaps it helped her forget her own decency. She was fundamentally lovely and clean, never meant to be the wife of a dealer in dope.

Outside the solarium a coarse voice scratched, "Hey you peepingtomsonuvabitch!"

Maybe if I hadn't been still a little shaky from the encounter with the brunette, I'd have jumped through the ceiling. But now it was too late to hurry. When I turned, I saw the heavy figure of a man on the lawn, bathed in the light from the doorway. It was the thick-set punk I had seen and overheard in the lobby. Huge muscles bulged under the business suit; hands hid inside patch packets, only stubby thumbs showing. He had black hair, a lot of it, and thick black eyebrows matching the deep black irises of his eyes. Even his knitted tie was black, *like a funeral director's*, I thought.

"Come here," he ordered, licking fat lips.

"I was just leaving."

"You don't dig out of this."

"Dig out?"

His thumbs wriggled. "Come here."

"Yes, sir."

As I took a slow step toward the door, he jumped outside the rectangle of light and disappeared beyond the doorway. I took two short, driving steps, lowered my shoulders, and broadjumped the door sill. That was caution. Something sang past my head and exploded on my shoulder blade. I landed and turned.

"Please," I stammered, "I'm only a stranger here and—"

A sap dangled from his hand. "You peeping sonuvabitch!"

Sucker, I thought bitterly, and waited. It doesn't pay to play easy with these boys.

He started toward me menacingly, an evil grin on his ugly fat face. I chopped down hard on his wrist. His fingers opened spasmodically, and the sap fell to the ground. In a second a switch blade gleamed from his hand. I had been expecting it. I moved in close and rammed his groin with a lifted knee. "I learned that in the army, sir." As his chin dropped, I clenched both hands together and hooked my double fist to the point of his chin. His fat face creased in agony. "The war was rather rough, sir!" My right fist lashed out and hammered his nose until it flattened. Blood spattered my clothes. He fell forward, and I chopped on the back of his neck with the edge of my palm, careful not to hit too hard. I wanted to knock the punk out cold, not kill him. He landed like a straw man, the useless knife blade bright in the light, and his strength leaking out with his blood into the damp grass.

He did not move again. They play rough in the dope racket, and I was glad I knew some of their tricks.

Straddling his inert body, I checked his wallet, ignoring the thick slice of dirty money. An identification card labeled him Peter Castille. Mr. Dalgren's information had named Castille Parente's strong-arm squad. Castille was thirty-six years old, the card said. I wondered if he had ever drawn an honest breath.

"You'll remember me," I muttered, and knowing his cop pal would investigate, returned the wallet.

The night was warm and not so dark as it had been earlier. A billion stars spangled the sky. They were real stars, not the synthetic sort strung along Broadway. The air had the bouquet of old wine. I'm a city lad, but there's a lot to be said for the country—if there are no Castilles and Parentes around. I padded through the pine trees and back onto the solidity of the lane. Only a dim square of light in the distance reminded me that a house full of sinister power hulked there.

As I lit a cigarette, I thought of Biz Parente's words: *I'm unhappy here. I need a strong man, like you.* Was that an invitation? I strode off along the dark lane, wondering if I'd see Mrs. Parente again.

CHAPTER TWO

T HE convertible waited atilt, one hubcap deep in the treacherous ditch muddied from an earlier downpour. From the direction of Parente's house, an engine throbbed. Wondering if someone had revived Castille, I unlocked the glove compartment. I chose a pocket automatic, not the heavier Luger. A .25 of foreign make, it was designed for close work. It had an overall length of four and a half inches and held six rounds. Don't underestimate this gun—it's unobtrusive in a pocket or it fits the hand; it's light and fast and deadly. The trick is to believe in your marksmanship and load the magazine with high velocity, center-fire cartridges.

I hid behind a tree across from the convertible. Headlights gouged a hole in the darkness under the trees. A speeding car slowed, and a spotlight winked on, impaling the convertible. The car inched forward. A man said clearly, "He musta been drunk as a skunk," and a girl laughed as their car gunned off.

I sighed with relief, leaned against the tree and waited. The thunder of a jeep, coming from the opposite direction, drifted in. One headlight tunneled around a bend and Willy Pickle slammed to a stop. "Mack, Mack! You here?"

His bulky body shot up above the jeep. Starlight flashed off a long barrel. "Mack!" A loud snick warned that the rifle was cocked and ready.

"Here, Willy."

Willy veered. "You in one piece, pal?"

"Always."

Willy stood spread-legged, a Garand in his big hands. "What you doin' in this neck of the woods?"

"I called on Parente."

"Doin' a job?"

"A big one."

"Anybody after you, pal?"

"Not yet."

"You're neck-deep in trouble, like always. That Parente don't joke, pal. Let's get the hell home." Willy stuffed the Garand in the jeep's holster. "See any dames at Parente's?"

"One."

"You try to make her?"

"Now, Willy."

"She dark and young?"

"Parente's wife. She's attractive."

"Mack, don't mess with his wife. Let's scram."

Willy maneuvered the jeep around, hooked a chain fast to the convertible and yanked it up onto the road. As he recovered the chain, I thought he was moving faster than I'd ever seen him. I trailed the jeep to the edge of town, followed Willy into a side road and out to the old highway. We came to acres of gardens and a roadstand wearing a sign, PICKLE'S PLACE. His headlights swept over rows of tulips and daffodils in bloom. In the night, the flowers were lovely, all muted golds and reds and whites.

At the end of a lane sat a bungalow, surrounded by a couple of elms, a single garage, and a greenhouse, off to the right by a line fence. We parked, and Willy joined me. "You old son." he chuckled. "Man, it's good to set eyes on you! How long was it since the last time?"

"Two years."

A switch snapped inside the house, and the porch lighted up. A girl stepped outside, and called, "You all right, Willy?"

"Sure, I'm always okay with Mack." Willy lowered his voice. "That's Wanda."

"The girl friend?"

"Sort of. Go meet her. She knows all about you, pal."

Alone, I mounted the steps. Wanda wore a man's short bathrobe wrapped tight around her body, the collar high at her neck. Her legs were trim. She was barefooted and bareheaded, a pretty, blue-eyed brunette, not over twenty-two.

"Hello, Wanda."

Her eyes hardened. "Try the motel down the road, Barry. The beds are softer." Her hard eyes leveled on my necktie. "Take your troubles and beat it, Barry."

Willy boomed, "Give Mack a kiss!"

"With the back of my hand," Wanda snapped. I wondered why she disliked me. At least, she was frank. You can travel a long ways with a spirited and honest woman.

Willy clattered up the steps. "Mack's on a trouble case. He met Parente's wife. Like I said, Mack's a heller with dames. Once in Honolulu he—"

The screen door slammed at Wanda's back. Willy rubbed the side of his face. "Now what made her mad, huh?"

He was my Willy, huge and sloppy in a work shirt and dungarees. "You never told me you were married."

"I ain't."

"What's Wanda's last name?"

Willy shrugged. "It was a funny damn thing, meeting her. It was last October and I was down to the stand and she come traipsing along in high heels and a tight suit and lugging a suitcase. She was very cute. She asked for a cup of coffee, see? I don't have none at the stand and we come up here. It was good coffee."

Willy grinned, not a dirty thought in his simple mind. "It musta been good coffee, pal. She's been here ever since. She didn't say what her last name was and I don't remember to ask. Let's kill some beer."

The kitchen was neat, scrubbed and empty. Willy opened bumper bottles of beer and we sat at a center table under a swinging light. We drank cold beer from the bottles and hashed over old times until Willy asked, "What's on your mind?"

"Sherry Dalgren."

"Knew you tailed some female. You ain't changed. Dalgren, eh? Heard the name before. That the Dalgren what owns a Midwood bank?"

"The same."

"His wife?"

"The daughter."

"Young stock this time." Finally, the name registered. "Hey, this Sherry Dalgren is dead!"

"Yes."

"I remember. They give her a whopping funeral. The papers said she died of pneumonia."

"Suicide," I corrected.

"Not according to the papers."

"Willy, I talked to her father. He showed me Sherry's suicide note written just before she took an overdose of nembutal. Sherry's story is not pretty."

Willy called, "Hey, Wanda! What happened to Sherry Dalgren?"

Wanda marched into the kitchen. She still wore the robe, but she had added makeup. High heels slimmed her trim legs. "Sherry died of an unusual virus infection." Wanda fetched another bottle from the icebox, sat at the table, and opened the bottle for herself.

"That's how this Sherry died," Willy offered.

"Nine months ago," I said quietly, "dope started selling in this county. Sherry was a senior in high school. A pusher started her on marijuana. Sherry got the dope habit, then switched to H, graduated to jolting, and ended a suicide."

"Talk English."

Wanda snapped, "H is heroin and jolting is pumping it into your vein. I don't want you to listen to his dreams, Willy. He'll get you into deep trouble. You have a home and business to think of."

She was Wanda-somebody and she knew the language of the rackets. I said, "What do you know about Dominic Parente?"

Wanda snapped, "He runs clean rackets."

Willy said he didn't know too much about him. "There's his horse betting and numbers and women. You know how it is."

"How did Parente acquire his string of taverns?"

Willy yawned and fetched more beer. "Some say Parente grabbed the gin mills for free when he climbed the ladder. I don't know and I don't care. I wanna drink, and it's always in the icebox, see? Get this straight, pal. This is my county and it's cleaner than most and Parente don't sell no dope. This Dalgren hire you?"

"Yes?"

"He must be a bluenose. You always raved about dope during the war. How the Japs used it and tried to get us to use it. Forget it, pal. No dope in my county."

"Well?" Wanda sneered. She swigged from the bottle, man-style. She was dainty, though, and always wiped the foam off her lips with the back of one hand while she measured me with her wise, young eyes, full of hate.

I took out my wallet, found a snapshot and laid that on the table. "A picture of Sherry before she got hooked."

They studied the snap. "Pretty," Willy offered. "Damned pretty, and healthy-lookin', too."

"It's the healthiest ones who go fast from a virus infection," Wanda said, studying the table top.

I returned the photo to my wallet. Sherry was young enough in experience to be this dame's daughter, I thought. She had blonde hair, clear eyes, and a frank smile. There was freshness and youth in her face, a new maturity to her body. Like most teenagers, she had too much curiosity. She had been too young to die.

"I'm tired," Wanda said, and her eyes when she turned them on me were sharp as stilettoes. "Willy, you better go to bed. Mr. Barry is staying at the motel."

Willy decided: "Mack stays here."

"We have only one bedroom."

"We got two. I can't turn a pal out to pasture at a cheap motel. Like cuttin' off my right arm."

"He'll get your head in a sling if you listen to him!"

"I ain't gettin' in this unless Parente sells dope."

"Parente operates clean rackets!"

"Mind if I make a phone call?" I asked.

Willy gestured at a wall phone, and as I waited for the operator to answer, Wanda jeered, "Do you want to be alone, Mr. Barry?"

"Lay off him," Willy said mildly.

I called Mr. Dalgren's number. "I hit town two hours ago, Mr. Dalgren. Your directions and information were excellent, but I need more help. They know I'm around. I'll keep in touch with you. Do you know who the fat cat is?"

Mr. Dalgren, after having the term translated for him, said he didn't know, but promised to look around. He wished me luck, and I replaced the phone. At the table, Willy asked, "What happened to you at Parente's?"

I told it tersely, omitting Mrs. Parente's love affair with the Scotch and her pass at me. Willy said proudly, "Ain't Mack a heller? That Castille is tough." Willy served more beer. "Wanda, you gotta like my pal. He can't bust up Parente, but he's the guy to give it a try. Mack, you better let the county cops handle Parente. We got a fine prosecutor, fellow name of Frank Crews. That tall guy with the drawl was Steady Eddy Flynn, chief of the county detectives."

"Steady Eddy?"

"A nickname. Eddy really guzzles the liquor. All the time he's got a load aboard. People say, 'Steady, Eddy. Don't fall on your face.' " Willy laughed. "The name is a joke, but Eddy's no joke. He's left-handed and quick with a gun."

"Did he arrest two dope peddlers recently?"

Wanda said, "The papers said they were grifters."

"Dope pushers," I corrected, and detailed Steady Eddy's conversation with Castille. "Your local law, headed by Steady Eddy, is stupid and crooked, Willy. Your county is wide open, thanks to some fat cat and the Steady Eddys. It's pretty much a rule of thumb that you can't run an open county and bar dope. A lot of the mob are old hypes. *Old hype* means dope addict and has nothing to do with age. The profit in marijuana and heroin is fabulous and the mob boosts the sales. But Willy, dope saps the guts and brains of any county. The pushers have no more morals than a toad. They start teenagers with gift cigarettes and the kids don't understand the danger. They smoke for kicks. Marijuana is—"

Willy slammed a bottle on the table. "Not our kids!"

"*Your* kids, Willy. After marijuana, comes heroin. H is costly, from three to five dollars a capsule. Where can the kids who are old hypes obtain the money for caps, eh? Well, the girls try prostitution. The boys try crime. Did you know that stickups and robberies have increased *three hundred per cent* in this county during the past year? Let me tell you how marijuana affects a kid."

"Not our kids, Mack," pleaded Willy.

"Yes, Willy, your kids. Listen. A few puffs on a reefer and your throat is dry, then you have to take a drink. Mix liquor and marijuana and all hell breaks loose. Restraint and decency fly out the window, even with the best people. Sometimes when the addict is *down*—that's slang for being off the stuff—remorse sets in. It did with poor Sherry Dalgren. Suicide seemed logical to her then." I leaned forward, not taking my eyes off Willy's stubborn face. "I've been with the police when they raided a joint where reefers are smoked. You wouldn't believe the degradation—mostly teenagers and the filthy pushers who have started them off." I straightened up. "I don't know about you, Willy, but I'd be happy to shoot anybody in the dope racket! If you know anything I can use to break up Parente's mob, give it to me. Just tell me and stay out of my way; I don't want you or Wanda in this thing."

"You're talkin' about New York," Willy frowned.

And Wanda sneered, "The boy evangelist with his popgun."

"Okay, be dumb solid citizens!" I pushed myself up from the table and dropped the automatic on the table. "This is *my* answer. I'm going after Parente and his mob pretty soon, and the gun talks the only language they understand. I won't get them all, but I won't *have* to get them all. I want the big boys—the swollen rats—*and* the fat cat who operates the green light!"

I stared at the gun and my fists clenched with fury. "This county is so good and healthy, basically. Not like *my* city, where the kids, some of them, never have a chance from birth. Out here you have the clean air, and the good, ripe earth, and at night you can see the stars, instead of just a soot-covered brick wall, when you look out of the window. You've got so many lovely things around you—like those beds of tulips. You've got healthy, pretty girls—like Wanda, here. Why don't you want to keep it that way, Willy? You and I learned in the army that you have to fight gangster nations with guns. Parente is a gangster nation on a small scale, but more deadly. He attacks from within, understand? Right here, somebody has to fight Parente or we go under. Believe me, no more Sherry Dalgrens are going to die in this county!"

After that outburst, I quieted down. There was so much silence in the kitchen that the drip-drip of leaking water at the tap was like the pounding of a sledge hammer. Willy should fix that washer.

Wanda said bitterly, "The moment you told me what Mack said on the phone I knew he was trouble for us. Don't listen to him."

"Mack don't never lie to me," Willy said heavily. "If I thought Parente sold dope I'd take that goddamn Garand I got and run out to Parente's alone and I'd—"

"Willy, Willy!" Wanda wailed. She swiveled to me, tears in her eyes. "Did they nail you at Parente's, Mack?"

"No."

"They can't trail you here?"

"I doubt it."

"You see? We needn't get involved," said Wanda, swinging back to Willy. "Please, it may turn cooler tonight. You'd better shut the greenhouse. Will you water my geraniums, too?"

"She's a nut about flowers," Willy offered. He patted Wanda's shoulder. There was a warm intimacy between them. His hand was gentle. "Sure, I'll water your geraniums, only you gotta be good to Mack and not fight with him, see?"

"Yes, Willy."

Willy yawned hugely. A gold tooth gleamed inside his mouth. "Damn glad you stopped, Mack." Willy went outside, and Wanda began to stack empty bottles under the sink. We had drained six quarts, and the beer hadn't taken any of the edge off her bitterness.

"Why are you worried?" I asked.

Wanda whipped around. The belt on the robe had loosened. Tanned legs shone for an instant, then she pinned the robe fast with the flat of her hand. "I don't care how tough you're supposed to be. You haven't got a chance to break Parente. You're only one man. One man can't buck an organization. Neither you or Willy together can buck this organization. I won't let you drag Willy into this!"

"I won't. Willy's the salt of the earth. But come on now, be a nice hostess. Stop fighting with me."

Wanda leaned against the table, which hit her in midthigh. "Why do you think I sent Willy outside."

"You tell me."

"So I could talk to you alone. When are you leaving for New York, Mack?"

"When I mop up Parente."

"Leave in the morning!"

"I never quit on a case."

"You've got to leave!"

"Got to?"

Wanda pounced on the .25. She snicked off the safety with a thumb. "You've got to leave for New York—in the morning!"

"Wanda, you're a big girl now." I stood up. "Close your robe."

"Go back to New York!"

"Why don't you turn off that broken record?"

"I'll kill you!"

"Your robe's wide open, Wanda. You're not wearing a thing under it either. Button it up or take a hitch in your belt or something."

I came around the table, and Wanda flared, "Don't touch me!"

"You know, you're a pretty swell kid. I like you and I love Willy, understand?" My hand closed over the gun and lifted it free. I set the safety and pocketed the gun. I had known that she dared not kill me, and she had known it, too. When I was close to her, I noticed the roots of her wavy hair. "You're really a blonde. Why did you dye your hair?"

"Leave me alone."

"Where did you learn mob jargon?"

"In magazines," she sneered.

"Are you hiding from someone?"

"No."

"What's your last name?"

"You inquisitive bastard!"

"Were you in Parente's organization?"

She slammed hard against me and sobbed, "They're killers, I know, but don't ask me how I know! Biz Parente is man crazy. She'll want a handsome guy like you. When she wants a man, she doesn't give up until she gets him! She'll be here tomorrow or the next day and she'll bring all of them down on us! I don't care what happens to me, but I'm not going to have anything happen to Willy!"

I patted her shoulder. "Nothing will."

She switched her attack. Softly now, "You're a heller with the women, Mack, a pushover for the right woman, Willy says. Mack, if you keep Willy out of this, you can have me." Her fingers were on my neck. As she kissed me, Willy's off-key whistle floated into the kitchen. Wanda grabbed my arm and dragged me into the dark corridor. She shoved me against the wall, and lifting on tip toes, she kissed me hard. "Just a token, darling." Her seeking lips were draining away my resistance. Her tongue was a darting spear, in and out, and I kissed her back and hated myself. She was Willy's.

As Willy stomped up the porch steps, Wanda pulled back. She whispered, "Take the last room on the left, darling. And remember, I never renege on a promise." She whisked into a room and closed the door softly.

From the kitchen, Willy boomed, "What happened to the party?"

"Wanda went to bed."

"Let's you an' me kill some more beer, okay?"

I hoped there was none of Wanda's lipstick on my face. "I'm tired," I said. "Call me early."

"I don't know why when you can sleep till noon if you want. Wanda show you the room?"

"Yes, and I'm hitting the sack. We'll drink some more tomorrow night."

"Sure." Willy sounded sulky.

I opened both the windows in the room and let in the cooling night air. Then I peeled down to my skin and flopped naked on the bed. There was nothing but sleep in the cards for me tonight, and I cursed the fate that had allowed Willy to meet Wanda first. She was a terrific hunk of woman, but whoever she was, she had been around, and she had been kicked hard. It had made her tough, and I didn't want her for an enemy. I wondered how much she knew about Parente's rackets. If only she'd talk, she might lead me to the fat cat. Where had she learned the patois of the mob? What mob? *They're killers, I know....* Her words had had the ring of sincerity. Oh well, maybe in the morning, in the sunshine ... darkness always made your fears seem bigger.

Later, Willy's voice rumbled questioningly in the next room. Then there was the answering murmur of Wanda. Shoes thudded, springs creaked and—that was their business.

Much later, after water had run in the lavatory, the house grew very quiet. A lucky guy, Willy Pickle. I wished I didn't envy him so much. One cup of coffee—and Wanda.

Sleep was coming slowly tonight. I was too busy pondering my progress on the Parente business. I had shot out of my corner too fast. When Parente got a look at the professional job that had been done on Castille, he might get suspicious and investigate. It was just possible that he might trace the phone call I had made from his house and trail me to Willy's.

There was a small sound outside my door. Then the door opened and a shadow drifted to the side of my bed. Wanda whispered, "Are you asleep, Mack?"

I lay still.

"Mack!"

"Huh?"

Wanda leaned down close to me, her hand fondling my cheek, her breath warm in my ear. "Mack, we don't have to wait. I know you'll keep your promise and not get Willy into trouble."

The poor kid—she figured if she smothered me with sex, I'd forget about Parente. And I suppose it could have happened if I'd let her. She wasn't being wanton, she was trying to protect Willy in the only way she knew. Willy was in no danger at the moment, but I was. I have as much biology as the average male, maybe more. Just then, Wanda was all biology, tempting as only a pretty, willing woman can be.

"Go away," I muttered.

"Don't you like me?"

"Of course I do."

Wanda sank down across my chest. I managed to lift her limp, warm body up, and rolling clear, slid from the bed to the safety of the floor. She stretched flat, waiting. *Had Wanda been a part of Parente's organization?*

"Mack, don't tease!"

"You shouldn't have come here. Go back to Willy where you belong," I said gruffly.

Wanda sat up suddenly. "If I do, will you go back to New York in the morning?"

"Ask Willy about me. He knows I never quit."

"And I don't tempt you at all?"

"You're very beautiful, and Willy's lucky."

"Come here."

"I'm trying to remember you're Willy's. Now beat it."

Wanda sat quietly for a moment, then she swung off the bed. "I love that big lug," she said. Then from the door she whispered, "Willy is my god. I love him."

She was gone with a patter of bare feet, leaving a large empty feeling inside me. *He's my god. I love him.* As I thought it over, her words reminded me of a lovely sound I'd once heard—cathedral bells pealing in the night. *He's my god. I love him.* A little like lighted candles by an altar, an island of sincerity amid the tawdriness of this county. I didn't sleep for an hour.

CHAPTER THREE

I⊤ WAS warm the next morning, and I put on my slacks and no shirt. In the kitchen, Wanda wore a white T shirt and garnet-colored shorts rolled as high as they would go. Her legs were still trim, but it was the T shirt that kept drawing my hungry eyes. Because there was no hurry, I lingered over a second cup of coffee. Busy as a housewife, Wanda jounced about until my scrutiny flushed her face.

"Mack, you stare like all men, but how come you don't whistle?"

"You should blush. When I'm in my bedroom, you keep *out* of my bedroom."

"I wanted to come into your bedroom."

"To stay?"

In passing, Wanda brushed her lips across my forehead. "I'm just no good, Mack. But let's not fight. Don't I look happy this morning?"

"I haven't forgotten the devil you were last night."

Wanda came back to me, and cradling my face between her hands, kissed me full on the lips. Stepping back, she grinned impishly. "I never renege on a promise. You know, Willy was right about you. Women can't help liking you. Do they spoil you, Mack?"

"Sometimes. Where's Willy?"

"Outside, cutting tulips for the market."

"Last night, you said you knew something about Parente. Why don't you give with the information? If you do, I can clean out Parente in a hurry and return to New York."

"I bluffed last night."

"You said they were killers."

"Did I?" Wanda smiled cryptically. "More coffee?" I shook my head. "Another sisterly kiss?" I shook my head. "We're going to be friends, aren't we, Mack. Please don't ask questions when I have no answers."

"Why are you so happy this morning?" I asked, wondering what she was up to.

She laughed gaily. "It was so funny to see you trying to fight me off!" She was like a playful kitten. Taking my hand, she led me outside and down a center path through the gardens. "Aren't the tulips lovely! Those red-and-yellow blooms are Keizerskroons. Like lifted fists, Willy says. Willy is poetic."

"You changed him. Who handles dope for Parente?"

"Some oily cluck named Tony Scales." Wanda waved at another bed of tulips. "Those are Pink Beauty."

"Where's Tony's headquarters?"

"Those flaming blooms are early DeWets. I think Tony hangs out at a tavern. Those daffodils are so pretty! What do they remind you of?"

"A little girl's yellow ribbon. What tavern?"

"The White Swan." Wanda's hand tightened in mine. "You must visit us in May, when the Darwin and Cottage tulips are in bloom. I can hardly wait! After the long winter, I'm starved for color and all this color turns me into a pagan. I want to dance naked down this path!" She glanced up archly. "Are you a pagan?"

"I will be, if you go into your dance. What's the White Swan like?"

"High class. I've heard there's some new place, much more important, but I don't know where it is or what it's called. You see, Willy changed me, too. He's so kind and gentle and—and lovable!" Someone came out of the stand by the road. "Hi there, Willy!"

Willy approached, lose-gaited, in clean work clothes. "Time you got up, Sherlock. How'd you sleep?"

"Some woman woke me up. She was nifty, too. It might have been a dream." I turned to Wanda, but she had walked off toward the bungalow. Willy stopped by a bed of glowing blooms, and using a knife, began to cut stems and stack tulips in a galvanized pail. I said, "You seem to like this flower business."

"Sure I do. It's fun watching what you've planted grow up, see? My uncle was a nut over flowers, and I used to help him out summers and vacations when I was in grade school. Remember how we used to chew about being partners in some business like this? Only I guess you're built for faster stuff. This gets dull, but what don't? Only it ain't been dull since Wanda come."

By the stand, a horn tooted. "Mack, go see what they want, huh? All we got is blooms at a buck a dozen."

"Yes, sir."

"Can you remember the prices?"

"I can, god."

Willy's brow wrinkled. "What's this with *god?*"

"A cathedral under the stars, bells ringing."

"Jesus, what a nut you are."

I went down to the stand and sold a woman one dozen blooms and left her buck in the till. Sitting in the sun, I waited for the Fords to pass. Over the space of a cigarette and some sun tan, a dozen cars passed, not one a Ford. I was about to forget the advertising slogan when a Ford rattled to a stop. A tall, lean man stepped out.

"All we have is tulip blooms," I sang out. "One buck a dozen. Will you take one or two dozen, sir?"

He ignored the sales technique and eyed me without a trace of amusement. "Where's Pickle?" he drawled, and his voice was faintly familiar.

My business brings me into contact with a lot of cops and this man smelled cop. That's no insult, but if he turned out to be left-handed and carried a load of liquor, he would be Steady Eddy Flynn, chief of the county detectives. And, Parente's man. I couldn't tell for sure because I hadn't seen the face of the man who had been with Castille. But the voice and the build checked.

I explained, "Mr. Pickle is cutting flowers."

Cold blue eyes measured my frame. "How tall are you?"

"Six feet." I stood up. He was just my height. "Or do you want it with the shoes off?"

"I want it with none of your horse manure. Weight?"

"A hundred eighty."

"Brown hair, brown eyes, and too much chin." He was checking against a description that somebody had passed along. I thought the chin part was his own idea. "Where were you last night?"

"In bed."

"All night?"

"Certainly." I lit a cigarette and blew smoke in his face. "Are you the local Gestapo or a stranger on a Cook's tour?"

"You a friend of Pickle's?" he countered.

"We were good pals in the army, but you wouldn't know about that. Did you fight the war from an armchair?"

"You're a wise sonuvabitch," he said.

Sauntering back to the Ford, he took something from the seat. When he headed back, he was busy slipping the thong of a sap around a skinny wrist and settling the butt inside his business hand, which happened to be the right at the moment. There was a possibility he was Steady Eddy, so I got ready to stab the lighted cigarette in his face if he started anything. He halted a yard from me and tested the sap against a thigh. "You know," he drawled, "this sap don't care whose head it busts in. Me, I like to call my shots. Who are you?"

"A citizen."

"Citizen, do you want to talk here, or do you want to get dressed and take a ride. Or would you prefer to ride off in just your pants?"

I said casually, "I understand that Dominic Parente has all the county boys on ice. I don't object to a certain amount of gambling, prostitution, and ticket killing in anybody's county, but how do you boys manage to close your eyes to dope peddling?"

"Well, I'll be a—" He stopped. It was too late to hit me with the sap. I had already hit him—with words. When he caught his breath, he said, "I don't know who you are, but if you're twice as big as you talk, you're still peanuts in my county. I'm Jake Tibbs. I count around here."

"What about the dope racket?"

"You a Fed?"

"A citizen."

His eyes had turned mild as the morning sky. A felt hat sat on his gray-thatched head. His neck needed a trim, but his shirt was clean, the necktie knotted carelessly. His eyes never left my face as he remarked, "You said *you boys*. That's plural."

"Of course."

"Just mention Jake Tibbs anywhere."

I said loudly, "Jake Tibbs." Not even an echo answered.

Suddenly Tibbs laughed. "By God, you're the man, all right." Tibbs stuffed the sap in one pocket, pulled out a buzzer, and flashing it cop style, cupped fingers around the edges. He was in no more hurry than a snail. I had time to read "Sheriff" and polish the badge before Tibbs hid it. "Sometimes I don't hear so good, mister. Did you say *you boys?*"

"Yes."

Tibbs sighed. "The sap didn't scare you and the badge didn't, either. Look, I drive a beatup Ford and you want it *you boys.*"

"Some rats are pretty smart."

"Look," Tibbs pleaded, "I rate me a county car and you want it *you boys.* Hellamighty, that Ford cost me all of a hundred fifty bucks, last October. It runs fine. It takes me any place I'm a mind to go and nobody says I can't go. I wanted to drive out to Willy's this morning." His voice had a plaintive sound, no ring of author-ity bulwarking the words now. "I guess a stranger hears all kinds of rumors about who's honest and who works with the mob. I don't know all the rumors, but I heard a juicy one this morning. You interested enough to listen?"

"Faintly." There was no more fun in this now than punching holes in a feather pillow.

"Last night, about ten o'clock, some man busted into Dominic Parente's private home. This man stole a diamond ring and two thousand bucks that belonged to a man named Peter Castille. Interested?"

"No."

"Castille passed out a description."

"Did he sign a complaint?"

"Well, this Castille is Parente's bodyguard." The blue eyes began to twinkle. "If Castille signed a complaint that said some-body busted his nose, split his chin, kneed his groin and so on, other men might get ideas and try their luck. Me, I heard the rumor and I'm curious. I got in the Ford and scouted around. There's a back lane past Parente's place where I run across a spot where a car had got mired in the ditch last night. It had to be last night because the heavy rain didn't start until seven P.M. yesterday and it didn't quit until after eight. The ditch and lane is mostly red clay and that mired car picked up a lot of that red clay. Tire marks showed where a car had backed around sharp, like only a jeep can. More tire marks said the jeep yanked the mired car to the road. Like I said, I'm naturally curious. Not many cars use that lane, mister. I trailed those car tracks and they fetched me right here. Knowing that Willy owns a jeep helped out no end. I'm wondering if there's some of that red clay on Willy's jeep tires, and if you drove a car, is there any red clay on your tires, too."

This was my first experience with a Jersey sheriff. This one understood the legwork of detection. "There's some red clay on my tires," I admitted, wondering what came next.

"Still, you might not be the man who stole Castille's ring and the cash. What about that *plural* remark you been making?"

"I might be wrong about that."

"Don't backtrack so fast, bub. Ask around. Just say Jake Tibbs anywhere. And, I'm not all-fired proud of my work. Anything I do, the next fellow can do. If the next fellow puts his mind and sweat to the job, and he won't need much mind or sweat, he can come here, too. You worried?"

"No."

"How's my friend Willy?"

"Fine."

"Wanda?"

I countered, "Wanda who?"

"I never heard Wanda's last name mentioned." I decided the blue eyes lied, and the mouth, too.

"How are you today?" he went on.

"Fine."

"We'll shake on that."

We shook hands and Tibbs twisted his wrist and glanced at the back of my knuckles. "Fresh bruises, you got there, bub. Name?"

"Mack Barry."

"Business?"

"On a vacation."

"Business when you're working?"

"Private investigator. I drove down from New York late last night and turned into that lane on my way to Willy's. When I went in to Parente's, I was only minding my own business. With my car stuck in the ditch, do you think I should have sat there all night and waited for someone to come and offer to help me?"

"That's your business. You on a case?"

I gave him the works. Softly I said, "She was seventeen years old. She was blonde and beautiful. The newspapers say she died of a rare virus, but we know differently. Interested parties say she was an old hype at seventeen and committed suicide. A lot of dope is peddled in this county. How many other thousands of kids do you think are hooked?" I paused. "I'm not going to apologize for sounding off to you, Sheriff, but while you were asking me questions, I was thinking of that poor kid."

Tibbs didn't look at me. "I knew Sherry," he said, and shook his head sadly. "Mr. Barry, if you nose into something, you might give me a buzz. Sometimes an outsider can dynamite where a sheriff is helpless. Even an honest sheriff who drives a beatup Ford. You figure to go after Parente and his mob?"

"Possibly."

"You got a license to pack a gun?"

"Yes."

"They can find you if they want to, Barry. And the next fellow who comes past might not be a friendly sheriff."

"Thanks for the tip. Finding me here was good police work. Who's the fat cat protecting Parente?"

"Anybody can mention a name, but you can't convict a man in a Jersey court because he has a name. You might try the White Swan."

Tibbs boarded the Ford and drove off.

I rather liked Tibbs. He was smart, but the question was: is he honest? Another question was: if he's honest, how much courage has he got? Tibbs was correct that they could find me here. Castille might come along. Or Steady Eddy Flynn, full of booze, a gun in his left hand. They probably had figured that I had been in Parente's hallway long enough to see and overhear things they didn't want noised around.

I could sit tight at Willy's for a while. I could unlimber my gun and nose around in daylight. Or head for New York. After a moment, I decided that since mobsters work mostly at night, I could take it easy, and I went back to where Willy was kneeling in the soil. "You're cutting a lot of flowers. Who buys?"

"Mostly florists."

"The White Swan a customer?"

Willy straightened and sat on his heels. Honest sweat was dripping from his face and soaking his shirt. "I heard the rattle of Jake Tibbs's car. What did he want?"

I told the story, with the tagline: "Is Tibbs honest?"

"Like the sun. We ought to get ready for trouble before it comes along, pal. I can park the Garand anywhere I work, but you either got to sneak back to New York or pack that little gun in your hip pocket."

"Right."

"Plannin' on workin' today?"

"No."

"You better spade up those empty beds. Do you good. That's fat around your navel."

"It's muscle. Speaking of fat, do you know any fat cats?"

"Wanda had a fat cat, but it lost a decision to a truck." Willy grinned. "Her cat was a tom and I called it Mack, after you."

I went up to the bungalow and went through the empty kitchen to my bedroom, where I hid the .25 in one hip pocket. When I re-entered the kitchen, Wanda was standing by the sink. In passing, I slapped the seat of her garnet shorts.

"Your fangs are long," she quipped, and made it sound so interesting that I hurried outside.

CHAPTER FOUR

B Y FOUR O'CLOCK, only one empty bed needed spading. Sweat rolled off my body. Muck stained my flesh and clothes. Every muscle ached. If this was what it takes to raise flowers, there wouldn't be any tulips to bloom in *my* garden.

An engine sounded. A Chrysler sedan drove up Willy's lane. A woman wearing a floppy hat sat behind the wheel. When she reached the bungalow, she sounded her horn. Wanda called out, "Hi, Ruth. Thought you'd never get here. The tulips are just right for cutting."

Chit-chat, I thought as I went back to spading. Presently, they walked along the path. Wanda aimed a generous quantity of hip and breast in my direction, but I remembered she was Willy's, and exciting as she was, she was not worth the loss of Willy's friendship.

Ruth asked, "Who's the new workman?"

"Some peasant Willy hired. He doesn't talk English. Hey, you! Say something nice to the lady."

I spat three choice Italian curse words over my shoulder. Wanda laughed. "He's a poor worker. Too much fat on his belly."

I flung more Italian words at Wanda, and both women laughed. I rested on the shovel and glared at them. Give or take a couple of permanents, I thought, this Ruth was around twenty-eight. She wore a low-necked black linen dress, sheer nylons and black linen pumps.

Ruth said, "I'd like to cut my own flowers."

"Cut all you want. They're a dollar a dozen, darling." Wanda snapped at me, "Make with the spade, peasant."

Instead, I watched Ruth.

Just beyond the bed of tulips I was working on, Ruth squatted on her heels. She held one knee higher than the other, and her dress was pulled tight across her shapely thighs. Not once did she glance in my direction. She snipped away at her tulips, and I studied her knees. They were nice knees. Between snips of the shears, her knees parted momentarily, and the peasant had a tempting glimpse of bare thighs. Finally Ruth straightened and handed Wanda a handful of tulips.

"They're lovely," she said. "I want more." Then she bent over, leaning across to reach blooms on the other side of the bed. The fullness of her breasts swelled into the V neck, and I had had enough of staring. I stabbed the spade savagely into the loam, while Wanda's amused laughter tinkled across the garden, insulting my bare back.

"That's three dollars' worth," Wanda decided.

"May I have the daffodils?"

"Anything Willy grows is for sale, darling."

Ruth passed by, and Wanda ordered, "Fetch the spade, peasant." I followed her to a row of glistening daffodils. "Dig a hundred plants, and don't break the stems. I'll get baskets."

"You want 'em dug in bloom?"

"Yes. Ruth bought them for fifty cents apiece."

I dug plants carefully. The bulbs had peculiar feeder roots, like tiny tubes. Wanda loaded two bushel baskets, and I grunted, "I'm in the wrong business. Fifty bucks for some weeds. Is Ruth going to plant them with a gold-plated shovel?"

"She's rich enough."

"What's Ruth's last name?"

"I call her Ruth."

"Do all the women I meet here have only a first name?"

"You haven't met her, peasant."

We filled the baskets. Wanda ordered, "Lug 'em to your car and load the boot."

"Why my car?"

"Because the selling price includes planting and Willy's on business. You follow Ruth home. Believe me, that will be a novel experience for you, following a pretty woman!"

I loaded the boot and followed Ruth. On the way, I figured it might be smart to wash the red clay off the convertible's wheels in case Steady Eddy Flynn or Pete Castille stopped around.

I cooled my heels on an expanse of neat gravel where tradesmen parked delivery trucks behind a ten-room house. I noticed a four-car garage. Besides the Chrysler Ruth drove, there was a convertible and an oil slick in another stall, so there must be at least three cars at this place. Ruth came out of the house, wearing loafers and a green dress with a row of large, white buttons down the front. She handed me one of two glasses she carried and ordered, "Drink this."

We drank. It was rye and water. Ruth was attractive, but she was a rich iceberg and I was merely a peasant.

"I plan to naturalize the plants before the sun wilts the flowers. Do you understand that?"

I shook my head.

Briskly she said, "When you finish that drink, fetch a wheelbarrow and spade from the garage. By the tool rack, you'll find a bag of bone meal. You can't miss the bone meal because it stinks and it's the only bag there. Load everything on the barrow."

I shrugged.

"You'll find a lavatory off the garage," she went on coldly. "Wash the muck off. You may be a peasant, but this isn't a muck farm."

Ruth swished into the house. I drained the glass. It was expensive rye. It patted my stomach, walked up my spine and whispered into my ear that I should relax. I loaded the barrow, washed off the muck, and felt better by the time I was halfway through a cigarette. Carrying a covered, wicker basket, Ruth marched out.

"Follow me."

She struck off into the sun, across a lawn big enough for a small-fry baseball game. We detoured an island of evergreens and covered more lawn. Ruth had a rhythmic walk, and the fit of her dress hinted that the figure underneath was remarkable. Presently we passed a precisely-spaced clump of maple trees and Ruth stopped near a summer house. I glanced back. Only the chimneys of the house showed.

Casually Ruth directed, "We plant the bulbs under those maples. We sprinkle bone meal at the bottom of each hole and work it in. Then we fill the holes with plants and dirt. Do you want to start working or do you want another drink?"

"Choice?" I grunted.

"Of course."

I'm used to guns and women, or drinks and women, not spades and women. "Drink," I grumbled.

In the wicker basket were two tall glasses and a cocktail shaker beaded with sweat. Ruth poured one drink. I took it. Quietly she said, "Sing out when you're ready to work."

She carried the basket into the summer house. It was a large affair with a pole roof, slatted sides, and vines so thick on the outside that I couldn't see her inside.

I sipped. This wasn't a cocktail, it was chilled rye. While the lady of the estate loafed, I drank, inspecting minutely every bush, copse, thicket, and tangle of rose-bushes. I decided this was a pretty lonely spot and went on with the more serious business of drinking. Two baskets of daffodils laughed in the sun.

Fifty bucks for those weeds? Hah, I should be in the bulb racket. I drank some more, and presently there were four baskets of daffodils grinned wickedly.

Peasant, see how easy it is to make fifty bucks? Meet sucker customers like Ruth-somebody. Have a girl at home like Wanda. Imagine a nice business and Wanda, too. I drained the glass. There were baskets of chuckling daffodils all over the lawn.

"Ready?"

I drifted over to the summer house and went in the open doorway without knocking. Ruth was standing near a glass-topped table with her back to me. Whoever owned this place must have as much money as Parente, I thought. Several chromium chairs sported colorful, fluffy cushions. There was a chaise longue, a bridge lamp, and a grass rug over the dirt floor.

Ruth said, "We'll have one more drink and—" She stopped.

"And?" I prompted.

"And!"

Famous last words.

Ruth lifted on her toes and pirouetted around. It was a graceful movement. She lifted her arms towards the ceiling, stretching like a lazy cat.

"My God!" I exploded, and Ruth smiled dreamily.

Every button down the front of her green dress was unbuttoned except one at the hem. Ruth shrugged out of the dress. It fluttered to the grass rug and she stepped free. Suddenly she came close to me. Her arms pinioned my arms fast and her lips took possession of mine.

Drunkenly I wondered if this exciting woman had lured me into a deadly trap. Everything was ready, the chaise longue beckoning, flat like a bed, with one pillow. I'm a fool for a woman, but not that big a fool.

I broke her grip and pushed her roughly down to the chaise longue, where she collapsed in a heap. Jerking the automatic from a hip pocket, I snicked off the safety and prowled to the open dorway. Nothing moved out there. I stole outside, and hugging the wall, eased to the corner of the summerhouse. Nothing stirred in the woods at the rear except a worried yellow bird. He bubbled music and hid inside a vine tangle. A man could get killed here and nobody would ever know. If Wanda still hated me, and Ruth had the proper connections with Parente, my grave might be this woods. There is no more efficient means to set a man up for the kill than a woman. Still wondering what was behind Ruth's metamorphosis, I sneaked back into the summerhouse.

Ruth stood by the table, her eyes wide. "That—that gun! I—I don't understand!"

I pocketed the automatic. "I'm the one who doesn't understand. Put your dress on."

"Why?"

"Put it on!"

Her face seemed to fall apart. "I—I get like this and—and I can't stop myself! For God's sake, don't torture me!" Her body trembled convulsively.

"Sit down," I snapped.

Ruth sank to the chaise longue. I draped the dress across her lap. "You weren't the least bit clever, Ruth. At Willy's you ignored me too completely. While you were innocently snipping tulips, you weren't very subtle about your come-on."

"Do we have to talk about it?"

"Every move you made was a calculated seduction, so I played along. It was fascinating, but what's the motive?"

Ruth flung the dress to the rug. Despite the tiny roll of fat across the white expanse of her stomach, she was quite a woman. But she ought to cut down on the calories.

"I know what I am and I know the one thing that brought me here, Mack." A vein in her neck pulsed with high voltage. "There's nothing in my mind but you. When I get like this, I don't care who the man is."

"How long have you known Wanda?"

"Several years."

"Where did you meet Wanda?"

"...."

"Why did you come to Willy's this afternoon?"

"Wanda phoned that the flowers were lovely."

"Did she mention me?"

Ruth hesitated a split second. "But I *do* like flowers! Any kind of flowers. I work hard with my flowers and I don't *have* to work." Ruth sat up and extended her hands, showing me the calluses. "I'm being more frank with you than I've ever been with any man, except my husband. I want you to understand what I know about myself. When I sense the approach of this uncontrollable mood, I work harder." Ruth shrugged in despair. "Work never relieves the tension. If you knew my husband—oh, he's no help! Always too much business and too many men friends and too much golf. Please help me."

"Not until you answer more questions."

"Pour me a drink before I faint!"

She was a nymphomaniac, or wanted to make me think she was. I slopped rye into her glass, started to hand it to her. She stared past me at the doorway and gasped, "Frank!" It takes a pretty woman to set up a man properly. If Frank had a gun, my grave beckoned.

Frank seemed to fill the doorway, but he had no gun. He was a solid man with thick graying hair, a moustache, dark eyes, and darker circles under the eyes. Fine veins mottled his handsome face, and his cheeks were too ruddy. His chin looked weak, but it might be just unfortunate bone structure. Maybe it had nothing to do with his character. He wore a yellow sport shirt, gray slacks with perfect creases, and expensive golfing shoes. He looked like Midwood's number one outraged citizen.

"I don't mean to pry into your affairs, Ruth," Frank said, "but you happen to be my wife. Please put your dress on."

My face reddened. I stared at the vines, unable to face either of them. If Frank had carried a gun and shot me, no jury would have convicted him. He added, "Your loafers, too." Then, "Perhaps you had better return to the house, Ruth."

Ruth moaned, "You were playing golf."

Frank stepped further inside. Ruth fled through the door. Her husband said, "I am Frank Crews and this is my summer-house, sir." His voice was tired. With an effort, like a man dazed from shock, Frank Crews shuffled to the table and drank from the glass I had fixed for his wife.

I'm no stranger in a boudoir and no angel, either, but I'm not one hundred per cent heel. "I'm sorry, Mr. Crews."

He didn't answer.

"Nothing happened, sir. She just had a crazy mood."

His shoulders sagged.

"We had two drinks, Mr. Crews. Nothing but two drinks."

As he turned, his name finally registered in my mind. He was the county's prosecutor. He was Steady Eddy Flynn's boss. *Why were this gentleman's hands tied so Dominic Parente could operate?*

"There is no point in discussing the situation further, sir," Crews decided. "Please go."

"Unh, unh. I work for Willy Pickle. Mrs. Crews bought those daffodils and the agreement stipulated that they had to be planted and that's exactly why I'm here."

"Very well."

I was cold sober. We planted daffodils, a strange pair of men: one county prosecutor whose sworn job was to control the Dominic Parentes and one private investigator who had been hired to get Parente. Crews was a patient, meticulous man. As if he were lecturing in a courtroom, Crews explained the history of the bulb industry. This lecture, any other time, would have been educational. It was sundown when we finished the job.

There was sweat on his face and damp spots on the yellow shirt. "May I ask you one question, sir?"

"You've been swell, under the circumstances."

"If I had not arrived—I mean—would you have—"

"I'm only a man and she *is* beautiful."

He smiled wryly, not looking at me. "Only a man and a beautiful woman." Crews did not seem to be speaking about his wife.

We returned to the house and I replaced the tools in the garage. Crews had disappeared, and I drove off fast.

I don't know what Frank Crews did when he entered his house. He had been a gentleman with me. I thought about the frustration in Ruth's marriage—Frank Crews was over fifty and lacked stamina for the job of husband. But even a younger, more virile man couldn't have solved Ruth's problem. A nymph's need is for men—many men.

I found Wanda singing in the kitchen of the Pickle bungalow. She explained that Willy was off on another job, that this was the busy season. She wore a sheer blouse, a full skirt and high-heeled pumps. Her face had the satisfied expression of a cat loose for three days on the Canary Islands.

"Mack, did you like Ruth?"

"Yes and no."

"You like women, and she's awfully nice."

"Yes, but you didn't plan the caper very expertly."

"Caper?"

"We were alone in the summerhouse when Frank Crews walked in. Nothing had happened, but Ruth wasn't exactly dressed." Wanda's eyes nearly popped from their sockets. "Last night, you tried to seduce me and discovered I had some scruples about trafficking with my best friend's girl. You wanted me to forget the Sherry Dalgren affair, but you couldn't make me, so you switched to Ruth, knowing she was lovely enough to arouse my interest, didn't you? You know Ruth is a nymph, and you figured she'd tie my hands. Ruth *could* tie my hands, but not until I finish with Parente. Not anything you do, young woman, or anything anybody else does can keep me from busting Parente. I'm not sorry for your selfishness, but you certainly put poor Ruth on a spot. By Christ, I ought to—" Before I did what I ought to do, I added, "Where did you meet Ruth?"

"Don't ask that!"

"Ruth talked. Where did you meet her? I'm going to force it from your lips."

"Please ..."

I dug fingers into Wanda's soft shoulders. "Where?"

"We were—were—" Wanda stopped.

I slapped her across the face. "Where?"

"We were call girls. In the organization. That was before Ruth met Crews. I stayed on until October."

It happens like that. Some of the call girls are smart or lucky enough to escape before the bloom of youth has faded and demoted them to a house where they have no choice and a horrible future. I'm no prude. It was none of my business what a girl's past had been, but I had a job to do. "I hope you're happy the way you suckered poor Ruth. I'm warning you never to try and stop me again. A girl died unnecessarily because of a vicious racket. She was too beautiful and too young to die. And Parente has a bill to pay, understand?"

I sat down on a chair, and grabbing Wanda, threw her across my knees. There was no fight inside her. She had soft buttocks, but my palm was on fire after I had paddled her good and set her on the floor. I started from the kitchen, and Wanda called in a choked voice, "I—I'm sorry!"

That made the mess lovely, didn't it?

I slammed the bathroom door so hard that the catch broke and I couldn't lock the door. If Wanda followed me in here, I'd drown her in the tub, so help me. I soaked in hot water and finished off with cold, but none of the heat inside me subsided. Biz Parente, Wanda, and Ruth Crews. If I met any more Midwood women, I'd choke them.

I shaved and dressed in a gray flannel suit, maize-colored shirt, red tie and white buck shoes. I left the pocket automatic in a hip pocket and combed my hair.

Wanda sat glumly by the kitchen table. "Do you know the name of the fat cat?" I asked her.

"No."

"Why don't you help me?"

"I can't."

"I'll find out. It does no good to knock off the punks."

"Mack, where are you going tonight?"

"Out."

"Will it be dangerous?"

"I've got my eyes open."

"To the White Swan?"

"Possibly. I can't tell you because you're up to tricks."

"Mack, they'll kill you!"

"Which would fix your worries. If my brains are quick and my fists fast, I'll come back."

"What was Frank Crews like?"

"He was a gentleman."

Wanda flared. "Gentleman! Do you suppose he met Ruth at a church social? How many call girls do you think Crews knew before he married Ruth?"

"If I'm any judge, not many girls and not very often."

I went out. Wanda's voice caught me on the porch. "Mack, if you don't go out, I'll tell you something!"

That's the trouble with a stubborn woman. To keep you on the leash, she'll promise anything. She'll lie and lie. She'll scheme and plot, and she'll laugh if she succeeds. Laugh secretly, that is. There was too much work ahead to loiter with a woman.

CHAPTER FIVE

I N THE White Swan, most of the bar stools were filled and many of the side booths were jammed. There were more women than men, and more noise and smoke than anything else. I sat at one end of the bar, where the light was dim. I had one rye under my belt and another on the way down.

An elderly Romeo on the right kept worrying a young blonde with, "You've had enough to drink," and the blonde kept stalling with, "One more for the road, daddy." It would be morning before Romeo lured *her* into a motel bed.

Someone had pointed out Tony Scales, who knew all about dope. He sat in a nearby booth—a glossed-over hood with oily hair, knitted black tie, and chalk-stripe suit with a two- hundred-dollar label. Three young punks guarded Tony. Each had the flat, deadpan look of the wise guy. They drank slowly from triple-shot glasses, and talked sparingly, lips scarcely moving.

Smartly dressed women of all ages eddied about the room. They smiled at Tony and fawned over the smug punks. *Kicks, darling. I met a gangster last night.*

Once America belonged to the decent people. It wasn't so any longer—the Mafia and the fat cats and the bribed cops had taken us over, and we weren't fighting back. The White Swan was a fair example of how completely we were dominated by them. It was one hell of an exasperating experience to know the degradation of this county and have to sit on the sidelines. I did a slow burn and glared at my drink. I wanted to crash into Tony's booth and feed those wise boys the hard fists and smoking gun, which is the only language they understand.

The long room filled up. Laughter, oiled by liquor, grew easier and more shrill. Somebody shoved between me and the elderly Romeo, who was still worrying the blonde. I wanted no part of the newcomer and stared at my drink.

A female voice said, "The usual, Mike." A bartender nodded and went to work. I concentrated on my drink.

The voice said, "Do you have a match?" Famous gambit at the bar.

"No."

I thumbed my lighter into flame and lifted the contraption. Why didn't the grifter mind her own business? Cool fingers steadied my wrist, and wisps of hair brushed my cheek. She wore an interesting perfume called Scotch Mist. The only reason I recognized the perfume was that an ex-girlfriend of mine in New York used the same stuff.

I grumbled, "When you finish taking my pulse, sister, I'd like the wrist back."

She dropped my wrist. "Trouble at home?" Famous second gambit at the bar.

"Don't bother me. I don't like punks."

Silence.

"Goddamn punks in tailored clothes."

Silence.

"Give a punk an inch and he bounces a tire chain off your jaw. After that, you kiss his behind in public. Is there any explanation why decent women, if they're decent, salaam to those four punks?"

After a short silence she murmured, "Isn't it your soliloquy?"

It *was* my soliloquy. The inherent weakness of soliloquy lies in the obvious fact nobody is in it with you. I was a little island of rebellion in an ocean of White Swan servility. The bartender delivered a drink to the dame, and I flipped a dollar bill in his direction. He waited for another bill, and walked off. He didn't bring me any change, either.

Two bucks for a grifter's drink. Thank you, Tony. How much do you charge for a reefer, Tony? What's the local price for a cap of H?

I was getting no place inside the White Swan.

The female said, "Thanks."

One of her hands lay on the bar. The nails were lacquered red. She wore a ring with an emerald stone as large as Dublin. What did a two-buck drink buy in the White Swan? She had a very flat stomach, sheathed by a sleek black dress, and a Marie Wilson superstructure, partly unsheathed. Then I took in one chin, two red lips, one high-boned cheek, and one deep black eye, and a halo of black curls, and I knew we weren't strangers.

"You again," I said bitterly. "Go away."

Elizabeth Parente pouted. "You horrid man. Why did you ignore me so long?"

"I liked you better last night. In the sweater."

"I'll run home and change."

"Wear the red slippers."

"Yes!"

"And those pink panties."

"Did you peek?"

"It was the careless way you sat when I first came in. How's the husband?"

"He's not feeling well."

"How did you get out?"

"I'm my own boss, thank you."

I sneered. "They're four punks in a booth."

"Are you really so tough, Mr. Watts?"

"If I'm bothered, yes, tough."

Mrs. Parente called, "Tony."

That was an unexpected development. Tony walked over and I slid off the stool. Tony drawled, "Hello, Biz." He glanced over at me, his eyes labeling me a customer standing at the bar.

"Tony, I want you to meet a friend who is just dying to make your acquaintance. Mr. Watts, Mr. Scales."

Tony's limp hand found mine. I said, "Nice place."

"Thank you, Mr. Watts."

"Nice crowd. So deprecatingly deferential."

"Only the best people, Mr. Watts." Tony lifted a forefinger. "Whatever the gentleman is drinking, Mike, and something for Mrs. Parente. How's everything, Biz?"

"Under control." Some secret sign passed between them; I wondered if I had been fingered. The drinks arrived, and Tony purred, "Any time, Mr. Watts." He seemed to be committing my features to memory. "Be seeing you around, Biz," Tony said as he walked away.

"Just how tough are you?" Mrs. Parente mocked.

"Ask Castille."

"You beat him with a club, he said."

"Castile lied. My knuckles are sore."

"His diamond ring and two thousand dollars?"

"Castille rigged that story. It was just an accident I stopped at your place. Castille tried to part my hair with a sap, and I've had too much training in the army to let him get away with it. What made him so jumpy?"

She turned the question with, "I'd like to believe you, Mack Barry. Really, I would."

So, they knew my name. She had fingered me. She rattled on. "I'll tell my husband that Castille lied. They found out your name and occupation."

"Tony knows?"

"No. You must trust me, darling." Her cheek caressed my shoulder. "They know you're staying with a man named Willy Pickle. They decided you must have heard too much last night."

"And?"

"At first, I overheard them talking about rubbing you out, then they decided to sit tight until you moved. You *are* a private investigator, after all, and they're jumpy."

"Tell them to leave me alone. Look, I turned off the Turnpike to reach Willy Pickle's place. I had a flat and I saw your light. What's there in that that anybody should get jumpy?"

"I don't know. My husband is a business man." *Sure, with a gun and fists.* "I want you to understand that I like you and that I don't like my husband or his business. I'm on your side. I covered you with Tony. Won't you let me be on your side?"

"If you want to."

We started on a third round of drinks. Biz murmured, "Such a crazy man, to tackle Pete Castille. Why did you?"

"I told you. I wanted to be left alone and Castille wanted to play rough."

"Do you like the White Swan?"

"No."

"Let's goof off to a more exciting place!"

"Does your husband operate this other place?"

"Probably, but I never asked. Are all handsome private investigators so inquisitive?"

"I'm like a bus man on vacation. Is there anything upstairs?"

"Offices, I think. Are you prying?"

"Look, lots of taverns have rooms for the customers upstairs. I'm a stranger. Does your husband run all the county rackets?"

"I don't know, I'm not interested."

"You wear the mink coats and drive the Caddy convertibles."

"For heaven's sake, stop being so insulting! I have stone martens and how did you know I drive a Caddy?"

"In the rackets that's standard equipment."

"Damn you!" She stood on tiptoes and nibbled at my ear. "Don't be mean to an unhappy girl, please. I'm a little tight, darling. Let's move to this other place."

"Do you need someone's permission?"

"I'm my own boss. I'll tell Tony I'm going home, not that it's any of his business." She talked to Tony. I left change on the bar for Mike, and when she returned, we pushed through the standees.

As we passed a booth, a woman called, "Hello, darling," and I turned. There sat Ruth Crews, hatless, mink-wrapped, and smiling. Ruth grabbed my arm possessively, saying, "I'll buy you a drink, darling."

"I'll buy *you* one when I come back."

"That's a promise, Mack Barry."

Tony Scales faced me in the next booth. His lips moved, stir-style. In the eyes of the punk next to him I read: *I'll remember you, Barry.* Ruth had fingered me innocently, and it didn't make any difference if Mrs. Parente had, too, except that I don't like women to lie to me.

"Jake Tibbs," I said loudly. Nobody bothered to say that Jake was an honest sheriff.

Mrs. Parente tugged me off, then stopped inside the rear door. "For a stranger, you certainly meet the women." Her upper lip curled. "Did you know that woman's a nymph?"

"Sounds interesting."

"Why did you shout that name, *Jake Tibbs?*"

"We bumped into each other this morning."

"Perhaps you shouldn't have met Tibbs. Darling, you weren't the least bit inquisitive about how my husband learned your identity."

"How did he?"

"Jake Tibbs phoned the information."

It didn't matter.

As we wandered out, she had a tight grip on my gun arm. From the tall eaves of the White Swan, lights flooded most of the parking lot. We stood just beyond the light. "Darling, we'll take the Caddy."

She steered me to the fourth car in the shadows, a hundred feet from the tavern. It was a sports Caddy, top up, with more chromium trim than the Super Chief. Leopard skins covered both seats. As Biz opened the door, an inside light brightened the cowl. "Darling, you drive."

Biz slid under the wheel and across the seat. The leopard skin snagged her dress and exposed her left leg to the top of her nylon stocking. It was an absorbing sight, and Biz was in no hurry to settle the dress back where it belonged. I forgot that I had a job to do and concentrated on taking inventory of her assets.

At my back, a man said, "Got a sec, Mr. Barry?"

He was one of Tony's young punks, and Biz asked, "What is it, Mario?"

"Some dame wants to talk to him. Only take a sec, Mrs. Parente."

We walked back to the White Swan. In the deep shadows where the main wall formed an angle with an ivy-covered addition, Mario stopped. "So it's a private eye from New York," he sneered, one hand poked inside his swollen jacket pocket. "What's on your dumb mind, chump?"

"Who wants to know?" My voice had a tight sound that should have been a warning to both of us.

"Upstairs for a talk, chump."

"Who says so?"

"Tony. And *this*, meatball." He whipped an automatic out of his pocket. Against the ivy, a splotch of white gleamed at the height of a man's shirt front.

"You fetched help along, punk. Who's the friend?"

"Come nice and easy or do I got to belt you?"

"Belt me, you greasy bastard."

Mario started carving up my chin with the butt of his gun. I grabbed his gun wrist and twisted it downward, sidestepping at the same time, forcing Mario between me and his playmate. Mario aimed for my groin with his knee, but I blocked the blow with my own knee. My free left fist slammed into his belly, and it felt as if it had penetrated to the wrist. As his arm went limp, I jerked his wrist upward with both hands, and the gun barrel laid his chin open to the bone. I tore the gun loose.

The punk in the ivy rushed up, a little late, and I slammed Mario against him. Then I smashed the gun butt against Mario's temple, and he left the fight in a hurry. As he slid to the ground, I charged over his body and hit the second punk in the ribs with my head. I snapped my head up—an old Irish in-fighting trick—and his jaw caught it with a loud crack. As he staggered, I nailed him across the teeth with the gun. I could hear the crunch of shattering teeth. The punk went down like a bag of wet sand. It had taken no more than twenty seconds.

They were just two young punks, too sure of themselves to last long in this game. You learn to work fast or you don't stay in one piece. I felt a little sorry for the poor bastards.

Two people drifted out the rear door and the elderly Romeo who had pestered the blonde asked stupidly, "Somethin' happenin'?"

"They're drunk," I said.

"Tony's boys, and bloody drunk," the blonde said, eyeing me boldly. She was safe with Romeo tonight, I thought, wondering if she wanted to play safe. Romeo dragged her off.

I prowled over to the lovely lady in the Caddy. The cowl glowed like a Christmas tree. A dance band played sweet music over the turned-down radio. Biz turned to me. "It didn't take you very long, darling," she said brightly. "What did the woman want?"

I glanced back across the hoods of three parked cars between the Caddy and the rear of the White Swan. I had to shift position to see the rear door in the shadows, but the two punks were out of sight.

There was a slim possibility that Mrs. Parente had been too busy with the radio to have seen the melee, and certainly she hadn't heard it from here, because there hadn't been much to hear.

"There was no woman," I said. "It didn't take long, either."

"What did Mario want, darling?"

"You set me up nice for them, baby. Next time, play it smarter. Park a punk in the tonneau. When I'm busy kissing you, the punk can belt me. That's expert advice. And, when you report to your husband, tell him to chalk up two more busted punks."

She was a cool customer. "What's that?"

"You're on your husband's side. You're a beautiful bitch who fingered me for Tony. Beat it."

Biz faced me squarely on the seat. "You are the most exasperating man I've ever met! What are you talking about?"

"Mario and another punk tried to take me."

"The stupid fools!" Biz leaned across the top of the door. "Are you all right?"

"Get one thing straight, Mrs. Parente. I don't give a damn whose side you're on, but tell your husband not to send any more punks after me. I'm on vacation and I don't like punks. You can keep your beautiful body home where it belongs and tell Parente if he bothers me again, he hasn't got long to live. In fact, I don't think he *does* have long to live, anyway."

Something I had said jarred her, peeled all the expression off her face. "You mean—my husband is dying?"

"He should have left me alone."

"Then you don't know—I mean—" Whatever Biz meant she didn't say. She fingered my coat and tugged me closer. Her red lips puckered and her eyes closed for a kiss. She was so treacherously beautiful and so obviously had me pegged for a stupid slob that I slapped her across the left cheek.

Tears flooded her eyes. Fingermarks whitened on the red of her cheek. She sat rigidly erect. Breath hissed between her even, white teeth, then she bit savagely into her lower lip. "Don't ever hit me again." Her voice was a tearing sob in the stillness. "You bastard, tell me what happened."

"Mario pulled a gun and his pal tried to help out."

"Damn their insolence. They weren't to touch you, none of them. Listen to me, you—you brute! I like you. I liked you the first time I saw you. You're big and you're handsome and you're tough and I like big, handsome, tough men. This isn't going to end here, broken and ugly. I won't let it end between us! But don't fight with me. Just hold me close, darling, and never let me go!" A single tear squeezed from the corner of her eye and slid across the white marks my fingers had made on her face. Her voice snarled, "Don't hit me again! Nobody hits me. If you do, I'll kill you!"

She was a lying bitch. I slapped her again. With my left hand, this time, across the other cheek. It made a brutal sound. Her head jerked sideways, and her mouth opened then closed with a furious snap. Pain and hatred distorted every feature of her once-lovely face.

I started across the parking lot, hating her. Her husband had exploited this county too long. A decent young girl had died so that a bunch of slick crooks could grow fat; so that Biz Parente could wear stone martens and drive a Caddy.

An engine caught. *She was no good.* An engine roared. *She uses her charms to help punks.* A gear whined. *A fifty-year-old gang leader bought her charms, Barry.* A high-powered motor shifted into high.

I spun around. I was in the dead-center of the lighted parking lot. The chromium front of the Caddy leaped from the shadows, hurtling straight at me. I faked to the left. The Caddy swerved with the fake. She was hunched over the wheel, like a stock car driver. I crow-hopped far to the right. She jerked the wheel and the Caddy tried to follow my body. The front fender swished past and brushed the seat of my pants. The long side of the car nudged me on my way. I was lucky—the rear wheel missed crushing my foot by the width of a toenail.

Gravel spat up at me as the Caddy thundered away and lurched around the corner of the White Swan, toward the fence that bordered the highway. There was the crash of metal on wood and then the Caddy hit the old highway and roared toward Midwood.

What had I said that had almost peeled her face down to the bone? *I don't think your husband has long to live.* That had been a shot in the dark, sparked by my anger and desire to kill Parente. *Don't hit me again.* I shouldn't have hit her a second time. I should have choked the life out of her.

It was foolish to stand here. My convertible was parked in the darkness at the far side of the White Swan. As I hurried over to my car, a shadow sat up on the rear seat. I opened the door, lunged in and swung my hands toward a white throat. I stopped just in time. The shadow was Ruth Crews.

"You want to get yourself killed, sister?"

"Darling, darling, it's me!" she whimpered.

"Get out of that back seat."

"Please, I want to go with you."

"Get off that back seat! Go home to your husband! He's a gentleman!"

"I don't like gentle men," she quipped.

"Get off that back seat, damn you."

Ruth stabbed one foot over the back of the front seat, and her long, slim leg followed. When she landed on the front seat, her dress was high on her thighs. She made no effort to pull it down. "See, I got off the back seat, darling!"

What would women do without automobiles to slide in and out of, I wondered. I opened the door. "Shove off, Ruth."

"Don't be mean to Ruth. Let's not go home, darling, it's too early for bed. Listen, I know an exciting place. Take us there."

I wanted to bite deeper into the Parente mob. *I know an exciting place.* Biz Parente had said that, too. Were the two women talking about the same place? "Who owns this place?"

"It's a new one of Parente's."

I slid under the wheel and slammed the door. Ruth crushed against me, arms and lips clinging. She tried to work her tongue inside my mouth. "Sit still or out you go," I said, easing myself free. Ruth tried to sit still, but her breath came in ragged spurts.

"Tell me about this exciting place."

"Wait."

"A new hot spot?"

"Of course."

"You seem to know more about illegal places than your husband."

"That's because I'm Ruth and he's only a lawyer, darling!" She chuckled. "He's soft-grained, too much of a push-over for any beautiful face. Particularly, if the face is younger than mine." She shrugged. "I'm glad you didn't go off with that Parente woman."

"Why?"

"Because I have you now!"

I started the engine. When it was running smoothly, I said to the backside of the White Swan, "I don't want a Caddy. This is a 1947 Ford with a shabby past. The top leaks in heavy rain. It burns up too much oil, but I sweated honestly for every dime it cost. By God, I don't have much, but what I have is honest and—"

Ruth kissed two fingers, and laid them across my lips. "I like you just as you are, Mack Barry. I'm proud to ride in your car. If you can negotiate the winding staircase at home, drive the Ford into my bedroom. Tonight or any night, lord. Let's drive off. This is my treat."

"I'm not broke."

"My treat, lord. Left, down the highway."

CHAPTER SIX

F IFTEEN minutes later we turned off the old highway onto macadam, and the convertible chugged along through woods and fields. The stars lighted up blank houses where honest men slept. We climbed a rise and dropped into a narrow valley, then rumbled over a wooden bridge, leaving the laughter of a running brook in our wake.

"Next right turn, my lord."

"Where are we?"

"Virgin territory belonging to Parente."

The road snaked through more woods until the headlights picked up banks of shrubbery, two fieldstone pillars, and a closed, wooden gate. The legend warned: CLOSED TO ALL THOROUGHFARE. TRESPASSERS WILL BE PROSECUTED TO THE FULL EXTENT OF THE LAW. Parente making threatening gestures with the law. It was almost comical.

A man slid out of the darkness. An indistinct pair of lips under a low hatbrim asked politely, "Yes?"

"We are Mr. and Mrs. Longwood," Ruth chirped, and laid a folded bill on my thigh. "From Asbury Park."

"Address, please?"

"219 Court Street."

Ruth nudged my arm, I relayed the bill to a ready palm, and the man disappeared. When the gate swung back, he called, "Switch to low beam and drive slowly, Mr. Longwood." He was more polite than a politician running for election.

The road S-curved to another closed gate where a second politician asked, "Name, please?"

"Mr. and Mrs. Longwood," I said.

"No lights, please. Straddle the white line and drive slowly."

I flicked off the lights. A luminous white center line glowed on the tar. "Those the only guards, Ruth?"

"There are more around the fence and I think the fence is wired to trip off alarms. It's difficult to enter unless you're vouched for. Very high class, really."

"The name and address was a code?"

"The password for the week."

"How did you know?"

"Heavens, all those questions. Relax. I asked Tony."

"Come here often, Ruth?"

"Only twice. The place has been open only a few weeks." Ruth placed a warm hand on my knee. "Are you the sporting type?"

"I like sports."

"This place will send you!"

The luminous line led us up behind a large square house, flanked with parked cars. There were a few empty spaces, and I chose one and parked nose-out, remembering you often have to leave in a hurry. From the methods of approach and the profusion of sleek limousines around, I sized this up as the county's top gambling spot.

Ruth led the way. Ten feet from the rear wall, we walked into the sudden glow of a baby spotlight. Either it was operated by a photo-electric impulse or the guard was wide awake. We must have passed inspection because a door opened into a square, dim anteroom. The door swung shut at our backs and locked with a sharp click. I fingered the wall and decided they were lined with sheet steel. When an inner door opened, we followed a corridor into a narrow room studded with padded chairs. The light was bluish, and eerie shadows leered from every corner.

Against one wall was a small wooden counter with an opaque window above it. I saw no one behind the glass, but a woman's hand appeared on the counter, palm uppermost. "Cellar," Ruth bubbled, and dropped a fifty-dollar bill on the palm, which withdrew. I received a metal disk in return, numbered 28. Ruth left her mink jacket, and the hand whisked it off. Let's say there were twenty-seven customers in the cellar ahead of us, that would mean Parente had grossed nearly fourteen-hundred dollars for the night. The cellar sounded like a gold mine.

"Hurry," Ruth urged.

"What's on the first floor?"

"Only gambling."

"Much action?"

"Not as much action as the cellar!"

A solid door opened for us. Soft music ghosted up a carpeted stairway, which we trailed to the bottom. A lot of money had been spent here. The air was fresh, suggestive of air conditioning. The corridor at the bottom of the stairs was ghostly with blue lights. There were closed doors along one wall, each with white numbers, the nearest 6.

While we ogled, a stunning young girl carrying a tray approached. She wore a diaphanous gown, tied at the throat and wrists with tiny ribbons, the flowing hem trailing about the girl's ankles. "Isn't she gorgeous!" Ruth whispered.

The girl wore an eye mask spangled with silver stars. I grumbled, "If I don't see her eyes, how can I tell if she's gorgeous?"

"Goose!"

The girl's gown had no more substance than the shadow of a spider's web. There was a lot of firm, young flesh showing.

"Your number, please?" the usherette murmured. I surrendered the disk.

"Follow me, please." That was a pleasure.

Off a shorter corridor, the usherette opened Number 28 and stepped aside for Ruth, who darted inside. I was in no hurry. When the girl had had enough of my up-and-down stare, she breathed, "Do you think I'm gorgeous, sir?"

"The gown says so. But you know, I'd like you better if this weren't so public."

She leaned against me and whispered, "Next time, come alone."

"Why?"

"I can slip off from work and join you, okay?"

"You've got a date."

Cool fingers patted my face and she went off about her work. I heeled the door shut from the inside.

An amber eye in the ceiling winked down at a night stand bearing a tray, one bottle and two glasses. A heavy drape closed off the front, dancing devils decorated the walls and a wide studio couch waited. So did Ruth. Ruth was a woman who always knew what she wanted. And now she was waiting for me.

"What kept you, darling?"

I shrugged.

"Like this place?"

"Give me time."

"Like me?"

"You know I like you."

Ruth kicked off her shoes and one bounced off the ceiling. "I like men!" Her arms wound around my neck. Without warning, she tumbled backward, pulling me down on the couch. "Wheeeee!" she said, and the word blended eagerness with exultation.

Every step and every hour brought me deeper into trouble, and yet, in this moment, there was time for only one thing. After all, I thought, in the age-old way, I'm only a man. That didn't justify it at all—it was only a bromide. And yet—oh well—I snapped off the ceiling light.

The amber light glowed weakly overhead. I was fully dressed and sitting on the chair; Ruth lolled on the couch. She was quite a loller. When the steady, soft music stopped suddenly and didn't resume, I asked, "What's the next attraction?"

"Floor show."

"I was just wondering what fifty bucks bought here that I couldn't get somewhere else without fifty bucks."

Ruth switched off the amber eye and tugged at a rope to part the front drape. A spotlight laid a circle of gold on the center of a dance floor. I could hear the buzz of many voices but the background of purple was so dense that I couldn't see anyone across the way. The soft music turned hot and the sound beat into our cubicle.

A female stamped into the spot. In tempo to the hot licks, she exercised every muscle. Hand clapping followed her strutting exit. The second girl pleased with a belly dance. The third girl did a strip tease in reverse. There were six girls, each with a specific talent, and a masked contortionist wearing a smile climaxed the solo numbers.

"Like it?" Ruth whispered.

"Nothing I haven't seen before."

I jerked the drape shut and Ruth protested, "I want to see all of the show."

I yawned. "The clientele may be high class, but the acts are so-so. Where do the customers come from?"

"All over, I understand. Someone at the White Swan said there were usually New York and Pennsylvania cars."

"What does Parente call the place?"

"Helldorado."

Parente had the originality of a burp at a clambake. "How does the word get around?"

"Word of mouth, mostly. Helldorado is famous."

"How heavy is the gambling?"

"I don't know, but someone said the wheels get the heaviest play. For heaven's sake relax, and light my cigarette."

I gave her a light, then the darkness closed around us on the couch. Fifty bucks a couple for this tripe?

"There's rye in the bottle," Ruth drawled. "Make mine rye on ice and not much ice. Let's have some light, man. We're alone."

Under the amber eye, I slopped rye over ice cubes and wondered if Dominic Parente had thought about blackmail. It would be reasonably simple to rig an overhead lens in each cubicle. With infrared rays, Parente might obtain some remarkable prints of the wealthy clientele in a sporting moment. Particularly, when some husbands arrived at Helldorado with other men's wives. Inch by inch, I checked the ceiling for a concealed lens.

"May I have a drink?" Ruth whispered.

Let's see. The height of the outside corridor was at least nine feet because this seemed like a big, old-fashioned house. The cubicle ceiling was seven feet, which left two feet of clearance overhead for a catwalk and crawling photographer. Maybe one of the ceiling panels lifted up.

"Where's that drink, man?"

Ruth was lying on the bed, the cigarette fire almost at her lips. She sat up, snuffed out the cigarette, and took the glass between fumbling fingers. She drained the drink, and I said: "You trying to drown, young lady?"

"Hits the spot, man. More of the same."

The fuzz in her voice was thick enough to scrape off. I had wondered about blackmail and cameras in this cellar, but here was the real racket, right under my nose! "Where did you get that cigarette?"

"On the tray, man."

"Who put it there?"

"Standard equipment. Relax, man." She was as relaxed as an empty glove, her eyes half-closed. "One for you, man."

The use of *man*—that's tea pad jargon. I should have caught on quicker.

I studied the cigarette on the tray and wondered how I could have missed the setup. The cigarette was brown. In the trade, this type is known as panatella or messerole.

The stuff inside is called a lot of things. The ancients labeled it hashish. Army generals dosed their troops with liberal amounts of hashish before a battle, to stimulate them into the murderous frenzies that led to the unspeakable slaughters detailed in ancient history books. Long ago, hashish had been Anglicized into the sound of *assassin*, which connotes a maniacal killer.

In less lethal doses, hashish is called marijuana and cannabine, depending upon the locale of today. In Harlem and on the West Coast, centers of the trade, it masquerades variously as locoweed, tea, muggles, pot, bush and grass. A cigarette is a reefer or joint. Smoking up a joint is obvious patois to the users, who are dubbed balls, which is the opposite of a square, a non-user. To a ball, a square is a dumb bunny with no sporting blood.

Marijuana derives from a weed of the hemp family. *Cannabis sativa* grows wild on any vacant lot, in a city park among the roses, on a square inch of dirt in front of the local precinct station. From a single plant, enough grass can be obtained to roll five panatellas or a dozen joints. Here's a weed which makes the profit from daffodils penny business. A few puffs and the throat burns like a concrete road on a July afternoon. The ball believes he gets a bang, a kick or a kite. If he hits the stuff hard, he's on a binge. Liquor cools the throat, which explained the function of the tray in Helldorado.

The ideas jumped through my mind, kaleidoscopic. Ruth squatted on the couch, the bottle in both hands. Rye gurgled into her throat and dribbled off her chin. I knocked the bottle spinning. "How long have you been hitting reefers?"

"Don't get so excited, man. I'm just a joy popper." She meant an occasional user, not a hooker, who has the dope habit. "Let's feel the bottle. I got need for the colored water, man."

"Marijuana and alcohol mixed," I said bitterly, and wanted to go upstairs, find Tony Scales and squeeze the blood from his snaky body. "Can you buy H here?"

"I'll ring for some."

"Don't bother. Do all the cellarites smoke reefers?"

"Maybe they come to watch the sights. You haven't seen anything, man. Wait till the amateurs get started on the dance floor." Ruth waved a languid hand. "Let's walk on the ceiling. Take off our clothes and sport." All this in a dreamy voice.

"Reefers are habit forming," I lectured.

Ruth giggled. *Giggling is another sign of indulgence.* "Don't be a square. Let the monkeys ride your back, man." Her body shook with silly laughter. "I'm careful of the stuff. I'll never get hooked."

They all say that at first. Ruth needed marijuana like a lake needs more water—she was a nymph. Marijuana has the insidious property of turning decent girls into pseudonymphs.

I took the cigarette, stepped into the brighter light of the corridor for a better look. Yes, this was a panatella. I hid the thing inside my billfold. If anybody doubted my word, here was the evidence of the dope racket, started nine months ago, that had led to Sherry Dalgren's death.

The usherette breezed around the corner, carrying her inevitable tray. It held a bottle, two glasses, and a napkin. The reefers were probably hidden under the napkin. "Anything wrong, sir?" she asked.

"No."

She sniffed the odor that had floated from our cubicle and smiled wisely at me. As she drifted off, I slapped her cute backside.

Inside the cubicle, there was a smothered sound. I wheeled and went in. A man with very broad shoulders was backed into the closed drapes. Bare, hairy arms clamped Ruth to his chest. Her bare feet kicked the air impotently as she raked her fingernails across his face. He backed deeper into the drape, and I dove across space, aiming for his legs. I came up with an armful of drapery. I shoved the drapes aside and stood up in the purple gloom. A fat woman bumped me off balance and wandered off. Dim figures staggered on the dance floor, but Ruth and the man were gone.

The soft music pounded on. A man shuffled past. He swung his arms, slapped his chest and exploded, "Wow!" *Wow's* echoed from the lips of other figures.

A young girl swayed up. She was half-dressed and wore no mask. She giggled and fell against me. "I'm high on a tree singing to the coconuts, man," she said dreamily. Her lips on mine were moist and warm. "What's happening in the joint, man?"

I wanted to help this young girl, but there was no time. She was as unaware of danger in her situation as a laughing baby on the edge of a cliff. Where was Ruth? I felt responsible for her.

I raged around the floor, bumping into soft, giggling bodies. I burst into closed cubicles and dashed out again. No Ruth. What I saw and what I heard on my journey was beyond description, I finally found Ruth and the man. The time lag had seemed hours, yet not more than a minute had passed.

He had Ruth pinned in a dark corner. One of her hands clawed at his bare back. I drove a fist into his kidney. He stopped pawing Ruth, and turned around. He was stoned, deep within the clutch of the grass, his face silly as he drifted inside his own little hell. He must have sensed some danger, because his hands balled into loose fists. He swayed toward me in the ridiculously slow, swinging gait of the stoned. For no reason at all, he laughed. I stepped through his loose guard and slugged his chin. He spilled to the floor.

Shuddering, Ruth crawled into my arms. "I knew you'd come. I didn't go with him, I didn't!"

"It's all right."

"I didn't want *him!*"

"Ruth, forget it."

I half-carried Ruth around the rim of the floor, avoiding the amateurs on parade. If blackmail were part of Parente's racket here, this was a good time for photographs. Once inside Room 28, I stood Ruth against the wall, worked the dress over her head and slipped her feet into her shoes. "Fix your hair," I ordered, putting on my jacket. I tried to shut my ears to the stupid noise.

"Do I look all right?" Ruth asked, laughing at nothing.

"Sure."

Ruth waggled a finger. "I want you, only you. Okay?"

"Okay."

She took a single step toward me, then without warning, she sprawled into my arms as if she had been kayoed. She *had* been kayoed, by Dominic Parente.

I carried Ruth upstairs and set her on the divan. At the counter, the hidden attendant handed over Ruth's mink and asked, "Do you need any help, sir?"

"Not any you can give."

We had no trouble getting outside.

A breeze had sprung up as I carried Ruth toward my car. The air had the washed sweetness of every summer night in the country. It was difficult to understand how people could leave this purity for a place like Helldorado, but—maybe it just takes all kinds to populate a great country.

Ruth slept quietly on the front seat. I left my shoes by the car and prowled off. From the outside, Helldorado was a square shuttered mansion two stories high, crowned by a flat roof and railing. As I contemplated the roof I thought what a good idea it would be to find Tony Scales and drop him off the roof to see if he was as tough as he was supposed to be.

I looked around. I found a lot of shrubbery, neatly clipped; a flagstone terrace and before heavy oak double front doors; a velvety lawn sweeping down to starlit woods; more shrubbery and more lawn; music seeping through from the cellar. Back at the rear, I hugged the wall and eluded the spotlight. I had learned nothing.

I found Ruth asleep in the car with her mouth open. I leaned against the door and waited. There was no hurry. Fresh air and sleep were the restoratives she needed. Nearby were some flowers in bloom, lilacs maybe, scenting the night. A drowsy bird muttered once then shut up and went to sleep. Far off on the macadam road, a truck labored in low gear.

When the spotlight winked on behind Helldorado, a man inside the glow called to someone in the anteroom. "See you later, feller."

The light went off and a shadow strolled across the parking lot. He stopped to light a cigarette, which gave me time to hide behind a nearby tree. Just as he passed the tree, I flipped a pebble in his wake.

"Yes?" he drawled, and inhaling, lit up a lean face. As he turned to see who was behind him, I jumped toward him and smashed my fist into his face. He staggered, and I caught him with my left hand. He hit the ground and never moved. That time there was plenty of anger behind my punch. I was sure the man was Steady Eddy Flynn, chief of the county's rotten detectives. Maybe he had visited Helldorado to collect the weekly ice.

Now it was time to leave. I followed the shining white line to the first gate, and it opened. I switched to dimmers. The second gate opened obediently. When they had your money, it was easy to leave. As the car nudged between the pillars, the politician called politely, "Goodnight and come again, Mr. Longwood."

A good exit line—goodnight and come again. I spit out the window.

When I carried Ruth up the winding staircase of her home, I saw no one. If there were servants, they minded their own business. The second door led into a woman's bedroom. There were twin crystal lamps at either side of a vanity, a Hollywood bed with a pink velvet coverlet, and several full-length mirrors. Clothes were carelessly draped over chairs, on the chaise longue, and on the wall-to-wall carpet. I thought it must have cost a mint to buy and furnish this house. How much could a successful lawyer make in this county?

Ruth had lost a shoe. If that was all she had lost, she was luckier than most people after a binge. I took off her dress and her other shoe and sat her on the tiled shower floor in the lavatory off the bedroom. Cold water hissed from the needlepoints. That did the trick—her eyes opened and she sputtered inarticulate noises. I shut off the water, and dragging her into the bedroom, rubbed her dry with a mammoth towel.

"Hello, man," she offered, smiling crookedly.

I hid her under the sheets and coverlet. Her eyes were red-rimmed, a sure sign that she had been smoking up the joint. She beckoned with a crooked finger.

Ruth was back to normal. I switched off the lights, tiptoed down the stairs, and drove home.

The bungalow was in darkness. As I walked up the steps, Wanda stirred from a porch chair. "You're home late."

"I'm over twenty-one."

"And not very bright. What sort of trouble did you get into?"

"Nothing to worry about."

"Two visitors just left, Mack."

"Anyone I know?"

"Two of the county's detectives, a stupe named Ortell and one by the name of Labcock. I handled it because Willy was snoring. They wanted to chat with you, but I said you had left for New York more than an hour ago and they didn't bother to tell me what they wanted with you. I said you'd gone to visit an ex-army pal, and they seemed satisfied. I heard Labcock say out by their car that they might pick you up with a radio warning. Who did you kill?"

"A couple of Parente's punks got in the way."

"Can we expect a visit from some of his boys?"

"I doubt it. Punks don't yell copper and they won't come here."

"What did the detectives want you for?"

"I knocked Steady Eddy cold."

Wanda moved in close. She wore the old bathrobe with the undependable belt. *"You hit Eddy?"*

"He doesn't know I did it. Probably that's why the detectives called, but they can't pin anything on me."

"Are you going back to New York?"

"Unh, unh." I didn't want Wanda and Willy to get in trouble, so I added, "Maybe I'd better try a motel for the night."

"And have Willy think I turned you out?" Wanda shook her head. "The detectives may be back tomorrow. We'll park your car in an old shed next door. Come along."

Without headlights, I drove to the shed. Then Wanda took my hand and led me back through a gap in the bushes. We passed close to the greenhouse.

"I hope Willy watered my geraniums."

"Want to check?"

"Not particularly." We had stopped, and she pressed close to me. "What do I get for helping you out, Mack?"

I kissed her forehead. "Mack, Mack!" I kissed her lips gently, and when her lips began to press mine, I stepped back.

"Chicken," Wanda whispered. I took her by the arm and we went into the kitchen, where she snapped on a dim light. "Drink?"

"Make it some cold beer."

Wanda fetched two bumper bottles and we sat down and drank. "Didn't you go too far, slugging Steady Eddy?"

"Not far enough. He's in thick with Parente. I ran into marijuana at that new joint, Helldorado. And where there's marijuana, heroin can't be far behind. Incidentally, why did you cover for me?"

"You're Willy's best friend."

"Only that?"

"I didn't like one of the detectives, Ortell."

"No other reason?"

"Mack, I'm not much good, but I draw the line on dope. When I was still a call girl, I heard the rumors; and when I saw the stuff around—reefers only—I called it quits and walked out—last October."

"My information from Mr. Dalgren said marijuana was first sold about nine months ago. Maybe Parente was getting money hungry, or maybe the fat cat got too greedy. What do you think?"

Wanda's face clouded. "All I know is that reefers were around and I got out. Then I met Willy. I dyed my hair to help me forget the old life. It gave me—well—sort of a new personality. Parente doesn't want me, probably never heard of me. Another man, a fellow named Dicky-bird Allison, handled the girls."

"Allison very important in the setup?"

"Merely a smoothie. The call racket is high class and the girls never make trouble. If you stay and you're satisfactory, you earn good money. If you don't measure up, or you get V.D., they simply stop calling your number. I was very careful and saved my money. Any time a girl wants to quit, it's okay. Ruth left and I walked out. Nobody's bothered me. It's that simple."

"Ever learn how Parente could operate so flagrantly?"

"No. I just had a job. It was as if I had two personalities. When I was with a man, I was just doing a job, not really being myself."

Sitting there quietly, drinking beer as though it were water, Wanda looked like a little girl, her past hidden and a pink ribbon in her brunette hair.

"Could Frank Crews be the fat cat?"

"Ruth says not, although we never discuss it very much. She says her husband is honest and naive, except that he likes young girls. Mack, the fat cat might be one of the freeholders. Or the top politician who sits behind the officeholders and handles the leashes. You know how rotten politics is. I think Crews keeps his eyes and ears shut. You see, he has a private law practice. A lot of legitimate business drops naturally into his lap, cases that wouldn't fall his way if he stepped out of line. He's done very well, financially. A year ago, he bought that big estate. They have two servants and three cars, and Ruth flings money around as if it were pebbles." Wanda stopped for a swallow of beer and wiped the foam off her little-girl lips with the back of her hand. "That's the way I see Frank Crews, a man in a soft spot with soft hands, who likes the money that drops his way because he's prosecutor and—oh, I'm getting all mixed up!"

"You're probably right. Crews doesn't dare make a move or his income dries up. There are ways to feed Crews what the smart boys tab as honest graft—income tax returns, property turn-overs, title transfers, and so on." I didn't think we were getting anywhere, so I asked, "Shall we go to bed?"

We stood up, and I said quietly, "You haven't told me all the reasons why you helped me tonight."

She smiled. "You big lug, do you know I made up my mind to dislike you sight unseen? You see, I'm with Willy all the time and all he talks about is Mack-this and Mack-that. I tired of hearing about Mack, the hotshot. When you first phoned and said you were in trouble. I was worried and I didn't want to see Willy get into trouble because of you. With you around under my feet, I couldn't keep on hating you. What I like most about you is the way you tackle something so much bigger and stronger and tougher than you are. You go in with both fists swinging, as if you could *win*. When you went off tonight, I couldn't sleep. I found myself pulling for you to win. You're like an Irishman, always battling for a lost cause." Her blue eyes widened. "Why, damn you! You *still* think you can win! "

"Just let me find the fat cat and I'm home free."

"See?" Wanda waggled her head. "You can't win, Mack. This is too big for one man."

She nudged me with her hip. There was no sex in the ges-ture, but there was something hard inside the bathrobe pocket. I reached in and pulled out a .32 pistol with a semi- long barrel and a pearl handle. Breaking the pistol, I swung out the hinged cylinder which held six live cartridges.

"One of Willy's guns," Wanda explained. "I wasn't sure who'd drop in next and I wanted to be ready."

I returned the pistol. "You're one swell kid and Willy is a very lucky man."

Wanda smiled wryly. "I hope he never finds out about my past and turns me loose."

"Willy likes you."

"I'll have to tell him about my past some time. But now we'd better go to bed before the neighbors start gossiping."

We separated.

I sprawled on the bed and wondered what would develop next. Biz Parente knew who the local fat cat was. If I gave her a big play, would she let slip a name? Which way would Dominic Parente move next? How would Steady Eddy Flynn react? Would Ortell and Labcock, the two county detectives, stick to my trail?

I broke it off. One more question and I'd sound like the announcer at the end of a soap opera.

CHAPTER SEVEN

NEXT morning, Willy was off attending to the flower business. After my late breakfast, Wanda packed the .32 pistol in her pocketbook, told me to stay indoors, and tripped down to the roadside stand. I phoned Mr. Dalgren and reported I had detonated more dynamite. Dalgren wanted to form a Committee of One Hundred. I didn't want any amateurs messing up the action and told him that the only kind of an organization that obtained results was a Committee of One. He seemed satisfied.

Within fifteen minutes, the inside of the bungalow bored me. I wandered into the open woods behind Willy's vegetable garden and sat on a log. There was a gray bird on a branch above me. She sassed me. I figured it was a *she*. When I discovered she was building a home in a bush by the log, I moved off. Beyond the woods, a man was cultivating a field.

I remembered that the glove compartment in my car was unlocked. In the compartment were a Luger automatic, some spare cartridges, some gum, and—strangest item of all in a glove compartment—a pair of pigskin gloves. I decided to lock the compartment to protect my property.

I passed Willy's greenhouse and stepped inside. Somebody had sprinkled Wanda's potted geraniums. From call girl to greenhouse girl, that was happy Wanda. Among a dozen other potted plants, I recognized one tuberous-rooted begonia, and this was the extent of my horticultural knowledge. The long benches held nothing but loose, dry dirt.

Beyond the greenhouse was a ragged line of bushes and some wild cherry trees, festooned with the nests of tent caterpillars. The field by the shed lay blank and green, only the shed roof visible over the tops of encroaching alders. By the highway was still another line of brush, hiding my convertible from the view of passersby.

A long-tailed, brown bird sang from the topmost branch of a tree leaning over the shed. I stopped and listened to a full minute of music. Then I moved forward and the brown bird winged off. His being there had seemed like a good omen. Wild things are usually mute if they know anyone is around. Outside the shed lay a litter of rusty cans, two blown-out tires, some broken crates, and a weathered oar with a split blade. I walked into the shed, and passing a stack of new crates, saw the convertible.

A voice said, "Take it easy," and I turned.

From behind the crates stepped two men in snapbrim hats. I had stepped into a neat trap. The nearer man carried a .38 positive in one hand, and he grunted, "That your car with the New York plates?"

"Yes."

"Mack Barry?"

"Yes."

"You stand nice and easy so you don't get mussed up, Barry. Labcock, do a check."

They must be Labcock and Ortell, the two county detectives who had trailed me to Willy's. Evidently, Wanda's lies had backfired when the dectectives discovered I hadn't returned to New York. Labcock edged around in a tight circle to my back, keeping out of range of Ortell's gun. Not that I had any ideas of jumping that .38. One of my bright ideas had already miscarried—I should have remembered that no one is so quietly patient as a couple of cops on a stakeout.

Labcock found the pocket automatic in my hip pocket. "Good little gun," he approved. "One gun, lieutenant."

Ortell asked, "You got a permit for that gun?"

"Yes."

"For the Luger?"

"Yes. Are you an officer?"

"Lieutenant Ortell, county detective. Let's see the permits."

I tossed my wallet to Ortell, who studied both gun permits, back to back in a case. He examined the photostatic copy of a private investigator's license, which was guaranteed by a ten-thousand-dollar bond. Before Ortell finished with the license, I was sweating. Inside the wallet was the panatella cigarette that I had taken for evidence from Helldorado. No hooker is stupid enough to keep any marijuana on his person. Possession of marijuana in any form is a criminal offense, and if Ortell wanted any hold on me that panatella was a passport to the county jail.

"He's Mack Barry and legal so far," Ortell decided. "Catch," and Ortell lobbed the wallet.

My eyes followed the path of the wallet, which was another mistake. Ortell rammed the butt of the .38 into my stomach and my breakfast turned over. "Sonuvabitch," Ortell said.

Labcock cracked the back of my neck with a fist and grunted, "You'll learn to keep your hands off cops."

Ortell kicked my shin, and my knees buckled. I fell to one knee. Labcock booted my fanny and I tumbled on my face.

"Not where anybody can see it," Ortell ordered, and before I could draw into my shell like a turtle, Ortell's shoe caved in two floating ribs. I drifted off for awhile.

When I opened my eyes I saw the dirt floor and a pair of brogans. My ribs ached like jumpy teeth, and they must have used my body for a game of soccer. I stirred.

Ortell said, "Barry ain't so tough as I was told."

All I wanted was my ribs intact.

Labcock offered, "See can you get up, Barry."

I raised an arm and shoulder. A rocket exploded in my brain. My hand hit the dirt limply, and Ortell chuckled. "The guy gets a big buildup and I drop him like he was a butterfly."

"Try your wings again, Barry," Labcock suggested.

Hanging on to the fender, I pulled myself up. I was terribly dizzy. I staggered, banged against the rear wall, and lost my breakfast. All I wanted to do was lie down and let Wanda ice my face.

Ortell asked, "Ready to talk, butterfly?"

"I want a lawyer."

"See can you hire one, butterfly."

Faintly, Wanda's voice floated into the shed. "Mack, Mack!"

"The dame that stalled me last night," Ortell grumbled. "She butts in here and I'll fan her behind with a board."

Wanda called a second time. We waited. I hoped that Wanda would give up her quest because I didn't want her or Willy involved in my trouble. Wanda's calls grew fainter and farther apart.

When she hadn't called for a full minute, Ortell began, "Where were you last night, Barry?"

"In bed."

"Don't start lying. Nobody knows I found your convertible and nobody knows I'm here, but us. I got all day to take you apart, see? Where did you go last night?"

"To a tavern, Mr. Ortell."

"Address me as *lieutenant*."

"Yes, lieutenant."

"What tavern?"

"The White Swan, lieutenant."

"Who was with you?"

"A woman, lieutenant."

"Never mind the title. What's her name?"

"Mrs. Elizabeth Parente, Ortell."

"I'll slug you, you bastard! What time did you leave the White Swan?"

"About eleven o'clock."

"Mrs. Parente leave with you?"

"Yes."

"Where'd you take her?"

"Nowhere."

"Why not?"

"We had a misunderstanding and she went home."

"Okay, I got you outside the White Swan, Barry. What did you do next?"

"I was restless and wanted some relaxation. I went to a place called Helldorado."

"Come again?"

Labcock said too quickly, "That's a new nightclub near Cross Corners, lieutenant. Very respectable, too."

"Oh. You go to Helldorado alone, Barry?"

"No."

"Who went with you?"

"A woman."

"Who was this next woman?"

"Ruth Crews." I watched to see how Ortell would react to the name of the prosecutor's wife.

Ortell dipped into one hip pocket and dredged up an iron claw. That's standard police equipment. The claw has a sliding bar on a single cuff and a hand grip. An officer snaps the cuff on a prisoner, grabs the grip and twists. The toughest prisoner turns docile and remains docile. It was interesting to watch Ortell fit the claw over his hand and aim it at me. It was also the most transparent display of police menace I've ever witnessed.

Ortell said, "Who did you take to this Helldorado?"

"Ruth Crews."

"Positive?"

I shrugged.

"Barry, lemme straighten you out. You can't stand behind no name. The info I got—and there's witnesses—said you went to this Helldorado with a twist name of Daisy Shaffer. She's been booked twice on a morals charge, but maybe you don't know that. Okay, you took this Daisy to Helldorado, danced and drank. Daisy passed out. You carried Daisy out to your car. Labcock, is that the way we got it?"

"Yes, lieutenant," said Labcock.

"Barry, what about it?"

"This Daisy was quite a girl. I thought she knew how to handle liquor, but you never know about a woman. Or don't you know about women, lieutenant?"

"Listen to me! I got you outside Helldorado on the parking lot. What'd you do next?"

I needed prompting. "What *did* I do next, lieutenant?"

"I wanna hear you lie so's I can bust your brains loose!"

I lied. "Daisy was stiff. I propped her on the front seat. I sat behind the wheel. Daisy snored. My Ford has a starter button on the cowl. I pressed the button. The engine started. I shifted into first and—"

Labcock murmured, "Didn't you have a party with her first?"

That was the only funny remark anybody had made and I examined Labcock with new interest. He was watching his fingernails, which were clean, more than could be said for Ortell's fingernails.

"We can't broil this too much or we won't have any steak left, lieutenant," I said. "I shifted into gear. I left Helldorado. I drove Daisy to her home. Where does Daisy live, lieutenant?"

"458 Rodney Street, Midwood. An apartment, 3D. But you don't drive right off from the parking lot, Barry. You hang around. Do you see a man come out the rear door?"

"No."

"A tall man?"

"No."

"Wearing a hat and smoking a cigarette?"

"No hat, no cigarette, no man."

Ortell's voice snarled, "Do you toss a rock at this man?"

"No."

Ortell jabbed a hole in the air with the iron claw. "You want this in the nose?"

"You must remember to hit me where it doesn't show, lieutenant. But you're not playing fair with the questions. What happened to the man?"

"You sapped him. You knocked him cold. He was important. You was the last man to leave Helldorado before this man left. You was the only man with a chance to sap him. Why'd you sap him, Barry?"

"I can't sap a man I didn't see."

"This claw says you did!" Ortell roared.

"If that claw talks—" I was feeling better. "Yes, if the claw talks, it's brighter than the dope who dreamed up this yarn. The yarn is so full of bugs a shyster could blow it apart with five questions."

"In *court*, you mean!"

"Right here, Ortell, the yarn blows up."

"You could be lucky. That yarn don't have to go on the blotter, see? *If* you cooperate. You gonna cooperate or do I work you over?"

I was thirty-two years old and pretty resilient. I must have recovered fast because I said, "If you're a good cop, and that's a question mark, you'll shake the lead out of your fat tail and do some legwork to find the man who hit the important man you say was sapped behind Helldorado last night. Personally, your yarn stinks. I don't know why you want to frame a stranger in this county, but you sure try."

Labcock murmured, "Well, well."

"You bastard!" Ortell shouted. "I'm gonna drive this claw through your guts until it comes out the spine!"

Ortell brandished the claw, took a single step. I feinted fast at Ortell, then with my shoulder low, shoved Labcock into Ortell. Ortell sputtered, "I'm gonna—"

It was beautiful. Wanda walked into the front end of the shed and drawled, "What are you going to do, plumber?"

Ortell froze. Labcock gaped. Wanda clasped a pocketbook under one elbow. The pearl-handled .32 pointed steady as the sun at Ortell's navel. Wanda added, "Somebody move, please."

Ortell tried to unfreeze. "Don't bust into this. I got you labeled. You was a call girl, right?"

"The verb should be *were*," Wanda corrected. "Mack, are you all right?"

"Yes."

"They kick you around?"

"No."

"When you told Ortell off, did you know I was outside?"

"No."

"My man!" Wanda grinned. "Do you want out?"

As matters stood, I had been prowling around in the dark. Ortell had crawled from the woodwork with a gun in one hand and dirty cards in the other. If I were to reach the fat cat, I needed a look at the rest of Ortell's cards. I asked, "Just what did you plan to do with me, Ortell?"

"Take you in for questions."

"Anybody made a specific charge?"

"We can hold you on an open charge for twenty-four hours and—"

"Who asks the next questions?"

"The boss."

"Which one of your bosses, lieutenant?"

"The prosecutor."

"Frank Crews?"

"Yes."

"Has Mr. Crews heard the Daisy Shaffer frame?"

"Well—"

They had to play it that way. Crews was a gentleman. I told Wanda, "I'll see the prosecutor. I'll drive my car and Labcock can ride along. If I'm not back in two hours, get a lawyer on the trail."

"If you're not back in two hours," Wanda promised, "I'll use this gun on—" Wanda's eyes wandered over Ortell. "Do you know Willy?"

Ortell nodded.

"Willy helped win a war. Willy has the scars to prove that. Willy likes me. Any time you remember I was a call girl, just remember Willy. Badge or no badge, you'll buy a new set of choppers after Willy finds you! Incidentally, Ortell, before you were appointed a county detective three years ago, what was your business?"

"I don't have to tell you anything."

The .38 inched towards Ortell's navel. "Former business?"

Ortell forced out a word. "Plumber."

"You were a plumber, which qualified you for a detective. Where did you learn police work, lieutenant?"

He sputtered, but no words came out.

"Everybody knows you took a correspondence course," Wanda mocked. "Mack, you're safe with a plumber."

Labcock joined me in the convertible. Wanda waggled the gun at Ortell. I liked that young kid. She had courage. "Take good care of my man," Wanda ordered, and Labcock said, "He does all right by himself, lady."

I backed the convertible out, tugged the wheels toward the highway. Wanda called, "I'll see you inside two hours or else. And about Ortell—he wasn't even a good plumber!"

I drove off, loving that kid.

At the highway, Labcock said to turn right. Later a left turn brought us into the residential section of Midwood. The sun was bright and the sky an intense blue. The houses had a substantial look. The lawns had haircuts, tulips bloomed, and azaleas flamed. On one lawn, three youngsters too young for kindergarten played with a toy balloon. At the corner, a teenage girl talked to a boy.

Marijuana bait?

I gripped the wheel so hard that the car veered and almost sideswiped a panel truck. "If you don't know how to drive, let me know," Labcock grumbled.

I took a deep breath and concentrated on driving. As we left Midwood and hit into the country, I asked, "Isn't Midwood the county seat?"

"No."

"Where is the county seat?"

"Between Midwood and Grove City. Both towns wanted the seat badly and the politicians made a deal. That way, both towns get an equal share of the patronage."

"Are there two rival sets of politicians?"

"No."

"Who's the county big shot?"

"The way you talked to Lieutenant Ortell gave me the idea you knew everything," Labcock snapped.

That wound up the quiz program.

With Labcock directing, we finally drove up behind a row of European ash trees and parked at the rear of an imposing pile of stone. Overhead were barred windows. There were other parked cars—three shiny black limousines with low numbers, and a prowl car.

"Before we go inside," Labcock said, "I want you to get one thing straight, Barry."

"Sure."

"That spunky girl was pretty excited when she first come into the shed, and I didn't like the careless way she handled that .32. I didn't want to have to jump her and you were smart not to squawk about getting kicked around. I'm civil service, see. I've been on the force fifteen years. I learned the ropes and I sweated over the textbooks and I took all the courses in good police procedure. Every damn course there was, I took. I'm still a detective."

"How does Ortell rate a lieutenancy?"

"In Jersey the politicians know how to circumvent civil service. Whenever a promotion was in the books, the word was passed downstairs which men were to take the exams. You damn soon found out which side of the bread had your butter. Maybe you don't like the preferential system, but it's a job and I wanted my family to go on eating."

"How did Ortell become a lieutenant?"

"Not even a plumber could miss. The job opened, the word was passed along, and nobody else dared take the exam."

Pretty, eh? It explained a lot of local chicanery. It was a partial explanation of why Dominic Parente held the county rackets in his palm.

I said thoughtfully, "It's tough for an efficient, honest cop to buck that sort of a rotten system. I didn't particularly like Ortell. It was evident he was a poor cop, but I never figured his background. Incidentally, you treated me rather decently."

"So what? You're an outsider, Barry. Here today and gone with tomorrow. Besides, the word hasn't gone around yet to cut you down to size, which can be done. I found out the score ten years ago when I was full of beans and wanted up the ladder. My name never came up, is all. Today, I take orders. All kinds of orders. That's my bread and butter, and damn little butter. Sometimes I come home from an assignment and I don't look in the mirror, but that's my business. I wanted to be a cop. I am a cop. That's why I want you to get one thing in your mind, Barry."

"Sure."

"I'm cop. I wear a silver badge that costs a buck wholesale. Ortell is a lieutenant and wears a gold badge, but that's not the only difference between us." There was no emotion behind Labcock's words, he was just giving me the facts. "If you handed me that line of crap you fed Ortell back there in the shed, Barry, you wouldn't be sitting here in one piece. That's because I respect the badge. *And*, I'm no explumber."

"I've got it straight."

The majority of cops I meet are pretty swell joes. It's the system that hammers them flat. Too often, cops wear invisible handcuffs. The politicians who give the important orders don't care about good police work. They're so interested in lining their pocketbooks they turn the police department into a cheap political club. The good cops get a runaround and the plumbers climb the ladder.

In this county, the fat cat politico had turned the county over to Parente, who had bribed enough policemen to keep his rackets going. Another thing—it's the job of the police to know what goes on inside their bailiwick. They knew all about Parente's setup, something that I didn't. What could the honest cops do to stop Parente? If they moved on their own initiative, they'd be tried on some trumped-up charge, convicted, and tossed out on their cans. No job, no pension for the years of service. Invisible handcuffs. If you ever wonder why the police cater to a Tony Scales and a Dominic Parente, just remember Labcock's story.

Labcock said, "How long are you sitting here?"

"Who's the local fat cat?"

"My aunt over in Grove City."

"Who's the bag man?"

"My second cousin."

"Okay, I'll cry for you in my beer."

"What the hell good are tears, Barry? Let's see if the boss does want to question you."

As we left the convertible, I wondered what Steady Eddy Flynn's business had been before he became chief of the county detectives. I thought of several appropriate words. Like *barfly*, for instance.

CHAPTER EIGHT

To see Frank Crews, I was piloted to the second floor and into an inner office, where a number of clerks at desks glanced inquisitively at the stranger. Labcock shoved through a door to a desk where the sign said, MISS ROHRBACK. She pushed an imaginary lock of hair off her face and asked, "Who is it, Lab?"

"Local Public Enemy Number One."

"I think Mr. Crews will talk to Barry."

News travels fast among the little people at county headquarters. I was hot in this county, and even Miss Rohrback knew that.

"Follow me, Mr. Barry."

We entered a corridor and turned a corner, and Miss Rohrback stopped suddenly. "Did you cream Eddy?" she breathed.

I grinned.

"I don't care if you did or not, Mr. Barry. I'm glad somebody creamed him! "

We entered another office. Across the width of a spacious room sat Frank Crews, servant of the common people. He smoked a pipe and wore horn-rimmed glasses. He was dressed like the successful man pictured on the business page of *Esquire* magazine. When Crews saw Miss Rohrback, he removed the pipe and glasses, stood up, bowed to Miss Rohrback and ignored me.

"Mr. Mack Barry, sir."

"Oh, yes. Thank you."

"I'll have the Shelldrank indictments completed in a few minutes. Shall I bring them right in, sir?"

"Please."

Miss Rohrback left. Crews remained standing until the door closed. Which shows how much of a gentleman the people had for a prosecutor. Miss Rohrback had a face as interesting as a folio page in a law book and a figure flat as an ironing board, but in this office she rated the full courtesy treatment.

"Good morning, Mr. Barry," said Crews.

He gave no sign that he recognized the man who had been with his nude wife in a summerhouse yesterday afternoon—and had been with his nude wife in Helldorado last night. I felt so much of a heel in his presence that I blushed and said, "Good morning, sir."

"Sit down, please."

I sat and folded my hands.

Crews parked behind the desk and studied an onion-skin report, the kind that a cop makes out. I've been around enough police headquarters to know that what Crews read was no more than Steady Eddy Flynn wanted him to know about what had happened outside Helldorado last night. Any cop on a ticklish job always asks a superior what should go into the report. I doubted that Crews read about the charge Steady Eddy had rigged against me. I felt rather sympathetic toward Crews. In this office, his hands were tied, either by the fat cat or untrustworthy subordinates—probably both.

Crews asked evenly, "Do you know why I wished to talk to you?"

"No, sir."

"It is my duty to explain the report I have received concerning you, sir. It is a report of assault and battery against the body of a police officer. No one has signed a complaint, but that is no guarantee that someone will not sign a complaint."

Crews leaned back in his swivel chair. He was handsome, in a dissipated way. I could picture him at the dinner table, after three

Manhattans, eating too much and then emptying a highball glass too many times. I knew why Sherry Dalgren's father had hired *me*. Frank Crews was too soft to stop Dominic Parente's rackets.

He went on quietly, "I must warn you, Mr. Barry, that whatever you say may be used against you. My chief of detectives, Edwin Flynn, answered a routine call last night at a new nightclub, the Helldorado, near Cross Corners. When Chief Flynn left, he was savagely assaulted with a blunt weapon. Prior to Chief Flynn's departure, you left Helldorado, Mr. Barry. You did not check out at the main gate until five minutes after Chief Flynn was assaulted. Do I assume from the time lag that you loitered in the parking lot?"

"I'm surprised to hear you say *assumption*."

"This is merely an interrogation, not a court of law. Did you loiter in the parking lot?"

"If you mean did I sit in my car, then I sat in my car for several minutes."

"Exactly how many minutes?"

"I don't know."

"Do you refuse to answer, Mr. Barry?"

"No."

"Do you wish to stand on your constitutional rights?"

"Look, according to your time schedule, some people had synchronized watches at Helldorado. I didn't."

"Do you wish to be represented by an attorney?"

"No."

"Did you see Chief Flynn leave Helldorado?"

"I do not know your Chief Flynn."

"While you sat in your car, did you see any man leave Helldorado to cross the parking lot?"

While I *sat* in my car? "No."

"Did you assault Chief Flynn with a blunt instrument?"

"No."

"Did you witness an assault on the parking lot?"

It was time to use my wits and take the offensive. I stood up quietly and stared down at Frank Crews. "I'm not going to lie to your, sir. I'm not going to refuse to answer your questions, nor evade them. I can say *no* again and again, but you might not believe me, and I want you to believe I had nothing to do with this assault on a police officer. You know I'm a private investigator?"

Crews nodded.

"Would you like a private investigator to solve this crime?"

"We have our own detective force, Mr. Barry."

"Did Chief Flynn recognize his assailant?"

Crews hesitated a split second, and I said, "Let's examine this from my point of view. I'm no stranger to the police in my city. And I have respect for the sworn duty of a prosecutor attempting to solve a crime. As a private investigator, trained at my own expense, I object to being used to prove or disprove a police theory."

I lit a cigarette and exhaled thoughtfully. "Let's examine this theory and the problem it poses for you. This police theory rules out hardened local criminals, prowlers, intoxicated guests with a yen to poke any policeman, and enemies; while it indicates that I committed an assault with a blunt instrument on Chief Flynn behind Helldorado on the parking lot during a starlit night. If you, as prosecutor, swallow this police theory about me, here's your *corpus delicti.*"

I ground out the cigarette. "You must place me on that particular parking lot in proximity to Chief Flynn. You must prove what blunt instrument I used and you must produce that blunt instrument as Exhibit A. You must prove that I, a stranger in this county, had a plausible motive for assaulting Flynn, whom

I have never met. If this case reaches the indictment stage, I'll produce a witness who was in my company all the time. She can swear truthfully, Mr. Crews, that while we were together in the car, she saw no man leave Helldorado, saw no man assaulted on the parking lot. You're a gentleman, sir. Is it necessary to drag this innocent witness into the interrogation now?"

"Of course not."

"With no complaint signed, would you let police reporters bombard this lovely lady with questions and insinuations?"

"Certainly not."

"I knew you were a gentleman, Mr. Crews. That's why I had to tell you the truth."

It was unfortunate that Crews was so much the gentleman. Gentlemen don't convict rats like Dominic Parente, nor break crooked cops like Steady Eddy Flynn. Remembering the Daisy Shaffer story, I suspected that the prosecutor didn't know my witness was his wife. As matters stood now, Crews had no case against me unless I confessed. I waited for him to struggle through the half-truths I had tossed into his mind.

"Mr. Barry, you've been in the county only a few hours. Why did you come in the first place?"

"Willy Pickle and I are friends. We fought a war together."

"How long will you visit Willy Pickle?"

"That depends on developments. Willy wants me to quit the private detective business and go partners with him in bulbs and flowers. I rather like Willy's offer. This is splendid, clean country, and I like out-of-doors work. Yesterday, I worked for hours in Willy's gardens. I'd like your opinion, Mr. Crews. Does the bulb and flower business in this county have a future for two men?"

"Why, yes."

"By the way, Lieutenant Ortell located me and appropriated my gun. It's a .25 pocket automatic, more a keepsake than a weapon. May I have it back, sir?"

Crews gave an order over an inter-office gadget. Then he stood and walked heavily to the windows. Out there were trees and distant fields, a stretch of blue sky, and a wandering cloud. I felt rather sorry for this befuddled gentleman who would be more at home riding that cloud to nowhere.

Crews talked quietly. This was a fine, clean county. Excellent towns. Progressive business men. The best of ordinary citizens. Wonderful schools, competent doctors, low tax rate. And so on. Had I noticed the prosperous dairy farms, the commercial orchards, and the fertile truck gardens, eh?

While the heart of this county burned to nothing, Frank Crews stood and rambled on like an enthusiastic realtor. He was still full of local chauvinism when Miss Rohrback tiptoed in, practically hurled the .25 automatic at me, and scurried out. I asked Crews casually, "Have you ever met a Miss Daisy Shaffer?"

"Umm, I think not, Mr. Barry."

"I understand she's a very attractive young lady."

"She's a local lady, eh?"

"She is, and I'm being introduced to her by a friend. You know, I may stay a week longer. Or accept Willy Pickle's offer." We shook hands. "It was nice meeting a gentleman, sir."

"Thank you, Mr. Barry."

"Thank *you*."

I wondered if he had forgotten about catching me yesterday afternoon with his wife. Not once had he hinted we had met before. When I went out, Miss Rohrback smiled. In the main office, two pert females wigwagged interest in my direction and the rest of the little people opened their eyes, cocked their ears and kept their mouths shut. I was Local Public Enemy Number One.

Downstairs, Ortell loitered by the exit door. He grunted, "The chief wants a word with you, Barry."

I followed Ortell to a pebbled glass door lettered in black, CHIEF, COUNTY DETECTIVE BUREAU. We went in, the door closed, and Ortell shadowed my back.

The office was a square, bright room with furniture so functional that the atmosphere was severe. A big, muscular man with cropped blond hair stood by double windows, arms folded across a wide chest. He had pale blue eyes and no eyebrows. He looked strong enough to break off my arm and flip it out an open window.

Steady Eddy Flynn sat at a desk. He wore two souvenirs of my fists—a mouse under the left eye and an agate on his chin. A snapbrim rode high over dark hair, and his lean face was sour. For a long minute Flynn and the muscular blond gave me the slow stare, until Ortell grunted, "He come apart easy in that shed, Chief, but he smiled on the way downstairs."

Flynn drawled, "Ready to go, Barry?"

"Yes."

"You're downstairs, now. No smart bastard saps me and walks off grinning. Read this."

Flynn flipped a newspaper clipping across the desk. I bent down and discovered that a jobless man, forty-six-year-old Jack Cable, had been found in a Grove City alley with a bullet hole in his chest. No date, no circumstances, and no obit. Of course, Chief Flynn was in charge of the case and had uncovered several hot leads which would be followed by an arrest at the proper moment. I glanced up.

"You know this Jack Cable?" Flynn drawled.

"No."

"Tell him, Pegler."

The muscular man opened a manila folder that lay on one windowsill and read tonelessly from an onion-skin sheet. " 'Upon examination, the bullet located in Cable's left lung was presumably fired from a .25 automatic, foreign make, with six lands, and a right leed directional fire. Comparison tests were run off in the laboratory on four bullets from a pocket automatic, a German Walther numbered 57348. The bullets proved identical under a comparison microscope.' Chief, do I show this wiseacre all the photos or is he too paralyzed to know the score?"

Flynn said, "Why'd you murder Jack Cable, Barry?"

I pulled out the .25 pocket automatic and sniffed the barrel. The gun had been fired recently. I broke open the cylinder and discovered five empty shells and one live cartridge. I said, not at all casually, "My gun is a Beretta." Flynn ordered, "Type a new report and make it a Beretta. Anything on your mind, Barry?"

The moment Ortell had taken my gun, I had walked into this. They had dropped the Daisy Shaffer angle and shifted to this new frame. I knew exactly what they had done—fired five bullets from my gun, which was registered with the New York police; shot comparison photos which recorded the agreement of the numerous microscopical ridges of the bore, the width and depth and pitch of the grooves, and the rest of the gun's individualistic characteristics marked on the bullets; substituted a bullet from my gun for the one located in Jack Cable's lung. I doubted that they had had time enough to accomplish all that, but just so long as they had five bullets from my gun they could do all those chores at their leisure. This made a neater frame than the Daisy Shaffer yarn.

I pocketed the gun. "Why pick on a stranger, chief?"

Flynn's eyes were half-closed. "You make just one more move in my county and you'll find out why. You use your fists once more or poke into somebody else's business and I'll toss you in the can so fast you won't hear the door clang."

Flynn opened his eyes wide. "You're not upstairs with a *gentleman*. You're downstairs with Eddy Flynn. You're nailed, Barry. Get the hell out before I sick Pegler on you and we gotta scrape you off the walls."

Pegler added thoughtfully, "We're an accommodating bunch in this county. If you want to do a Dutch in here, Barry, you still got one cartridge in that popgun."

I turned and managed to bump against Ortell. Ortell grinned like the pet tomcat with all the family's goldfish in its belly. "We got a brand new morgue, too."

I fumbled the door open, turned. "Chief, what was your business before you headed the detective bureau?"

"I've been a cop for seventeen years. Do you want to snoop back any further?"

No, I didn't want to snoop any further.

I went out and remembered you always close the door softly at police headquarters. I went out with my fists reduced to fingers, blanks in my popgun, and my brain full of butterflies. Last night and all of yesterday and the night before had been mine; today and tomorrow belonged to Steady Eddy Flynn, crooked cop.

Outside this pile of stone, I was surprised to see the hot sun high in the blue sky.

CHAPTER NINE

I wENT up the bungalow steps and into the kitchen. At the table sat Wanda and Willy, attacking a leaning tower of hamburgers, a heap of fries, and schooners of beer. "Heard you had some trouble this morning, Sherlock," Willy sang out.

"Yes, and Wanda bailed me out."

"Some girl, huh?"

"She certainly is."

Wanda asked, "Hungry, Mack?"

"Only for a glass of beer." I sat at the extra chair and helped myself. Wanda asked, "How did things go with Frank Crews?"

"He was deepdish apple pie. So I'm not hungry."

"Don't kid me," Willy mumbled around food. "I can tell you're in the grave again. What happened?"

"It seems I killed a man."

"Huh?"

"It seems I killed Jack Cable."

"Who's this Cable?"

Wanda tumbled first. "Oh, they're using a different frame from the one this morning?"

I told what had happened in Crews's office and downstairs with Steady Eddy, and added, "This frame can't stand up in a court and they know it. If I move, they can dump me in jail, so the frame ties my hands so I can't move."

"Left you a bullet to do a Dutch," Willy said, and chucked. "I warned you about Steady Eddy. Drunk or sober, you shouldn't have slugged him."

I sipped beer, Wanda picked at food, and Willy's moon face stitched in concentration until he said, "That Frank Crews give up too easy. He dummied up and fed you to Steady Eddy for the frame."

"Crews wasn't in on either frame, it's Steady Eddy's brainwork. Everything crosses his desk before it reaches Crews and nothing reaches Crews that Eddy doesn't pass along. It's possible for a top officer to insure a racket and grab the graft. I once thought the fat cat was a politician, but now I think Steady Eddy's the one."

"They *really* peddle dope in my county, pal?"

I showed him the panatella I'd carried in my wallet. "Ruth said reefers are standard equipment at Helldorado, but heroin you have to order."

"A cigarette like this started Sherry Dalgren off?"

"Yes."

"And she switched to H and did a Dutch, eh?"

"That's the way it was, Willy. If you'll let me stay here for several days, I may think of a way to shake off that murder frame."

"You stay," Willy decided, and stalked to a corner where he unloaded a Garand rifle. "Had the rifle ready for Parente's boys if they come here." Willy put the rifle back in the corner and hid the clip in a drawer. "I knew you couldn't lick this organization alone, tough as you are. Let's not cry baby. We can transplant annuals for the cut-flower trade this summer. You know a zinnia from a marigold?"

"Marigold stinks, right?"

"You flunk, pal. The new hybrids smell sweet."

Willy wandered out, Wanda stacked dishes. In my bedroom, I changed to shorts and dropped the pocket automatic on the bureau. It was a good gun, light and fast and deadly, but they had me licked. I phoned Mr. Dalgren, said I had to keep quiet for several days, asked him not to start a Committee of One Hundred, suggested patience, and hung up.

I told Wanda, "Even the Committee of One is a failure."

"It was too big for one man," Wanda sympathized.

"Unh, unh. I was careless. I'll dream up a new angle."

"I might think of an idea."

"If you do, forget you thought. This isn't for amateurs."

I joined Willy in the garden. There's no art to transplanting zinnias. Peg a line, trowel holes, set in a plant, tamp it loosely. Do that a hundred times, and Willy grunts, "You're a helluva farmer. Look at the cow's-horn row you got."

I planted another hundred zinnias, and Willy mused, "You always went in too fast. In the Pacific Theater you called it your intuition. Me, I got to turn things around and around in my mind because a guy that can't think fast has to give his brains a long workout. Maybe my way is safer and smarter than the way you work, pal."

"Don't tell me how to be a detective," I said sourly. I planted until my back muscles ached and my knee joints creaked. Willy had his talents, mostly muscular. The only goal he had reached was this daily back-breaking knee-creaking routine. I did all right. I was only fifty zinnia plans behind Willy.

We finished, showered, and ate Wanda's grilled chops, baked potatoes, tossed salad, and cherry pie. As we sat on the porch afterward in the deep twilight, the phone rang. Wanda answered and returned to say, "Ruth's coming over for a visit."

I stood and yawned. "It's bed for me."

"If you're not here, Ruth will be disappointed."

I went to bed anyway. Ruth would always be disappointed to find the man of her choice in bed without her. I didn't remember dozing off, but when I awakened, the luminous hands on my watch said it was ten minutes past one. Willy's door was closed, so I stole a bottle of beer at the icebox and hid in a deck chair on the porch.

I had finished two cigarettes and the beer when a sedan pulled up behind my convertible, and Wanda said clearly, "Thanks a lot, Ruth."

"You helped us a lot," Willy agreed, and the sedan drove off. As the two neared the porch, Wanda asked, "Do you think we helped?"

"You're damn tootin'," Willy grunted, and seemed pleased. He stumbled noisily on the steps and Wanda hissed, "Don't wake Mack. I don't want him to know we were out."

When the house was quiet, I barefooted to bed. It was two o'clock and another day, not mine. Sometimes you can't earn a slug to cheat a gum machine.

When I confronted Wanda at breakfast time, she said coyly, "You're to phone Midwod 4700 immediately."

"Anyone I know?"

"Call and find out."

I phoned, and Biz Parente said frankly, "Mack, I want you to meet me on the back lane in an hour."

"Okay," I decided, "but no tricks with a Caddy."

Biz murmured, "That was only because you slapped me."

Wanda's eyes were full of question marks, and I said, "I've got a date."

"Yes, with Biz Parente. The operator's a friend of mine. She told me who 4700 was."

I went outside and watched Willy weed flowers. If anybody ever again mentioned gardening to me as a vocation, I'd do a Dutch. Presently, Wanda called from the porch, "Mr. Landers said to come dig those year-old azaleas. He took our price, thirty bucks the hundred."

"Load the jeep and we roll," Willy crackled. "Mack, that's a big deal. We sell azaleas next spring for a buck- fifty in bloom."

"Why doesn't Landers retail the plants and make the big profit?"

"Hell, he's only a wholesaler"'

They loaded the jeep with boxes and two spuds, which are sharp, narrow spades. "We'll be back in a couple of hours. Have fun with your date," Wanda jeered, and the jeep roared down the lane.

I changed to slacks, T shirt and white bucks for the date with Biz Parente. Driving the back lane, I noticed the ditch where my convertible had got stuck the other night and started me on this run of deep trouble. I parked near the break in the bank, and a couple of minutes later, Biz Parente walked the aisle under the conifers and hopped to the road.

"Good morning," she offered coolly. She looked neat and trim in a dark green sweater, yellow shorts and loafers. She slipped into the front seat and displayed her lovely legs, voluptuous body and inscrutable black eyes. She was beautiful, when she wasn't trying to kill you with a Caddy.

Biz said, "Big eyes on the wolf this morning."

"The better to see all of you, my dear."

"Are you sorry you slapped me?"

"That was a stupid mistake."

"Don't ever use force with me, Mr. Barry, and we'll click." She bounced primly on the cushions. "If I navigate, will you drive?"

"Certainly. Does your husband approve of this trip?"

"There are some things I'm allowed to do without supervision and please don't start any tiresome questioning routine. This is for fun. The first direction is drive straight ahead."

I couldn't drive straight ahead on this lane. It was like Biz Parente—full of curves.

High among the lonely hills, the little lake was a sapphire studded with an emerald circle of trees. There was a white stretch of sand of talcum powder delicacy, two Indian birch canoes, and a dock with a three-meter board. Off the dock was a spacious cabin with a screened porch that jutted out over the water.

I put on swim trunks and sunbathed on the dock while Biz executed neat back flips, jackknives and swan dives. After a while I called lazily, "Don't you ever tire of diving?"

Biz paddled to the dock and stood beside me. "May I have a cigarette, please?"

It was difficult to light two cigarettes and admire Biz. She wore two scanty pieces of white-dotted green cotton masquerading as a bathing suit, and no cap. I finally lighted the cigarettes, and taking one, Biz stood feet far apart, tanned and relaxed. She asked a question that I had wanted asked for an hour.

"Hungry?"

"Let's eat the rocks."

Biz pulled me to my feet and we went inside the screened porch. It was cool, and cluttered with expensively casual furniture. The huge, main room off the porch had two fireplaces, a timbered story-and-a-half ceiling, leather furniture, pictures of hunting scenes backed by knotty pine walls, heads of assorted big game animals, and a thick rug for wading.

"Do you want to towel?" Biz asked.

"I just want to eat."

"I'll be with you in a moment."

Biz left. From the moment we had arrived at this lush Parente retreat, Biz had maintained her aloofness, not once inviting a kiss or hand-holding or any other intimacy, except via the swim suit.

Why had she brought me here? *To relax*, she had explained. *You're in trouble and you must forget it for a while.* I didn't forget my trouble, but I planned to play along and see what developed.

When Biz returned, a white terrycloth robe swathed her body, with the collar fastened high under her chin, a button at work across her breasts, a belt double-knotted over one hip, a second button busy over one thigh, and the hem flowing around her open-toed sandals.

I protested, "That robe is unfair to an interested spectator."

"Didn't you *just* want to eat rocks?"

The kitchen gleamed with chrome trim, waxed linoleum, white and gold tie-back curtains, a mountainous refrigerator, a deep freezer unit, and the too many other gadgets deemed necessary in the modern kitchen. "You're my guest, sit down," Biz ordered, and I sat on a leather-padded bench beside a cherry table that must have cost at least a hundred bucks. It would be a shame, I decided, to ruin this Parente luxury, if I ever got around to making any inroad into Parente's luxury.

Biz tossed a salad with the expertness of the Waldorf's chef, set a mouth-watering steak inside the electric broiler, and sliced slabs of crusty bread. "Shrimp cocktail, sir?" No, the guest decided. "Fries?" No, ma'am. "Dry or buttered bread, sir?" I chose dry. "Pickles, olives, celery hearts, sir?" No. "Name anything, sir, and it's in the pantry or the freezer." I named nothing. "What about beer or liquor, sir?" The guest chose beer.

Biz brought a sizzling steak to the table. "There, sir!"

"May I carve that steak?"

"You may. And hurry!"

We sat across from one another and ate shamelessly. There was no conversation, no interruptions, no unnecessary movements. Afterward, we sat idly and smoked two cigarettes apiece. It was four-thirty.

"I'll clear and dry," Biz suggested, "if you wash."

We split the chores, like a happy married couple. It was four-fifty by the clock. Biz asked, "Swim?"

"I liked you in the green suit, but I don't want to swim."

"Very well. I'll have to leave for home soon."

I took her in my arms, gently, the way she wanted it. I kissed the pout off her lower lip. She remained perfectly cool and reserved. I let her go and offered lamely, "A man should kiss the woman who cooks so well."

"And we should dress and leave," Biz answered. In the central corridor, Biz said, "The lavatory is that way," and I entered a plumber's paradise. The face in the mirror sulked.

As I passed along the central corridor toward the room where I had left my clothes, Biz called, "Free for a moment?"

I trailed her voice into a cool, shadowy room with a Hollywood bed. Biz waited by the windows. "Over here." I went over. The buttons on the terry robe were still buttoned and the belt still double-knotted. "Listen."

In the shrubbery high at the window sill, a bird was bubbling music, a waterfall of sound. "So beautiful," Biz murmured. The bird sang several choruses, flew off, and started up again from a distance. Without a word, Biz turned and laid her lips against mine. There was no reserve in that kiss, nothing but dancing flames. She drew back, eyes challenging, and whispered, "You're the man I need."

My fingers were thumbs on that top button of the robe. It simply refused to unbutton. I gripped the ends of the collar and yanked, and two buttons arced across space. "Don't say I didn't warn you," said Biz huskily.

Somewhere outside the cabin, a bell-voiced bird sang three notes. I lifted on one elbow, and at my side Biz stirred. It was twilight, and we had forgotten to go home. Biz murmured, "What's the fuss?"

"Only a noisy bird."

"We've loads of time, darling."

I kissed her lazily without bothering to reply. Suddenly Biz said, "I think we should talk, now that we've really got acquainted. I heard them talking about the frame. I know you're in trouble, bad trouble. That's why I brought you here—so you could find out what I'm really like, to offer myself as a helper. Do you want to get out of the frame?"

"It *is* a frame. Nobody likes a frame."

"There may be a way out. If you're strong, and I know you are, it shouldn't be too difficult. One thing you should know, my darling. I love you. I do not surrender myself to anyone, as I did to you. You should know that they're afraid of you. That's why they worked the frame. Because they're weak and afraid, understand?"

"I hadn't guessed that."

"They're afraid of a panic. If I help you escape from their trap, what will you do next?"

"Return to New York in a few days."

And leave me to—to—" Biz shivered. Her fingers laced with mine. "Take me with you, my darling! Now that I have you I'll never, never let you go! Please, listen to my story. I never knew my parents. I was reared in an orphanage, and eight years ago, I ran away. First I was a model, then a showgirl in a chorus line. I was only twenty when I married Parente, not knowing what he was. Four years of hell, my darling!" Her hands were strong, her body warm to the touch. "Four years I've waited for a strong lover to free me. If there's a way out of this mess for both of us, will you take the chance?"

"I'm not afraid of risk."

Biz lifted her searching lips to my face. I didn't know if other men, besides Parente, had had her, and strangely, I didn't care.

"Wait, darling," she reproved. "He's old, understand? I need you at my side for the long road ahead. A man like you can topple him from the throne. Then, you'd be *boss* of Eddy Flynn." Her soft lips explored my face.

"With you on the throne, we'll have plenty of money. We'll go abroad. In a while, we'll vacation in the Lido, or Paris, the Riviera, anywhere we want to go together." Her words sang inside my head. "You and I will be free to do exactly what we wish. Please, my darling, say you will take the chance!"

I said I would.

"First, you must topple him from the throne."

"How?"

"One mighty shove and the throne is ours!"

It couldn't be that simple, I tried to reason. I managed to sit up. Her arms refused to let me go. "Biz, I don't know how well you've planned this. We must reason it carefully, step by step. You say he's old and weak and afraid, but he has experience with the rackets, and gunmen on his side. How do I take over?"

"You must trust me to know his weaknesses. Never forget that they are afraid of you, no matter how many of them there are. Be tough with them and gentle me. Always gentle me, my darling?"

"Yes."

"Is a million dollars worth fighting for?"

"You bet."

"Am I worth fighting for, even if there were no million dollars?"

"Yes."

Her arms tightened. I must not use force with her, only she with me. There seemed to be a terrible hunger building inside her. "The rackets have—well, slipped away from him. There's no strong hand on the reins because he's old and afraid. Yet, he has position, power, men, and the money. All that can be ours. But you must believe that from the moment I saw you, I loved you. I wanted you. Now I've had you here and I always want that with you, my darling. I can't tell you exactly how we'll do it, but— tomorrow is Saturday; the rackets are brisk, then. No one will be at the house but him. Come to me later. Tomorrow night, say at twelve o'clock. I'll wait in the solarium."

"And it's easy, eh?"

"So easy for you with my help. You'll come?"

"I'll come tomorrow night at twelve." *A million dollars, and Biz Parente, all mine. Some guys get all the breaks, because they're tough.* "At twelve," I said softly. "In the solarium. Like the first meeting. Only better."

"My darling, my darling!"

It was after eight o'clock before we squared away and left the Parente cabin alone inside the hills.

CHAPTER TEN

U NDER the dome light at the kitchen table, Willy Pickle and Wanda faced two quarts of beer and two empty glasses. "Where the hell you been?" Willy growled. "Just when we got to have you around, you're off with that Parente tart. You make her, chump?"

Willy's eyes were bloodshot. A lump bruised his left cheek. Dried blood streaked his workshirt. Wanda's eyes were red-rimmed from tears. Her fingers slowly shredded a paper napkin. "Wanda, you tell it," I said.

Wanda sobbed, "We're sunk."

"Some pal you are, you tomcat," Willy charged.

"Wanda, get on with it," I said.

"Mack, our plan backfired!"

"What plan?"

"After you went to bed last night, we hatched an idea with Ruth to help you. We drove over to Helldorado and visited the— the cellar. Mack, I never dreamed it was that awful!"

Willy cursed. "Right in *my* county, the bloodsuckers."

"Mack," Wanda continued, "there were three reefers in our cellar room. Remember you said that Steady Eddy was the fat cat?"

"That was yesterday, but tell the rest of it."

"We had decided to put the issue squarely up to Flynn. Willy took the three reefers to Flynn. Willy told how and where he got them. Willy gave Flynn twenty-four hours to close down

Helldorado and run the dope peddlers out. Twenty-four hours, Willy said, or he'd go—"

"This was last night?" I interrupted.

"Last night. Close Helldorado or Willy would go to the newspapers. Flynn told Willy that he didn't understand how dope peddling could happen in his county. Flynn said heads would fall, that he'd get action for Willy. He thanked Willy for the evidence."

Willy growled, "I shoulda killed the louse."

"So," Wanda went on, "Ruth drove us home. This morning you ran off with Biz Parente. We went for azaleas. At eleven o'clock, we returned home and Flynn was waiting. He had Lieutenant Ortell, that blond cop named Pegler, and another detective. Flynn said, 'Kiddies, I said last night that heads would fall, that you'd get action. Come out to the greenhouse and see Exhibit A.' The six of us entered the greenhouse. Mack, during our absence, somebody had filled our benches with marijuana plants!"

"I got Ortell," Willy said, "before that Pegler sapped me. I coulda cleaned out the four of 'em with your help, tomcat."

"I prompted, "Wanda?"

"Flynn said, 'Kiddies, we've already taken a dozen pictures of this greenhouse. It's evidence that you two are in the marijuana business. Would you like to take some of those pictures with you when you go to the newspapers?' Mack, what can we do now?"

"In *my* greenhouse," Willy moaned. "Come see."

While I had cavorted in the hills, this home had burned. When crooked cops run a county, that's the way it is. Upright citizens get trouble, not the mobsters.

In the greenhouse, Willy switched on the lights. Yesterday, when I had strolled in here, those benches had been empty. Now, hastily planted marijuana weeds, some of the leaves wilted, covered the benches. The mob must have a marijuana farm near by.

"We'll get the stuff out of here, first," I said.

We filled two bushel baskets with weeds, built a bonfire, and burned the deadly stuff to ashes. Willy said, "Next?"

I had gotten them into this trouble. If I had stayed at a motel, Willy and Wanda would still be leading unruffled lives. I said as much, and Wanda answered quietly, "We're not sorry you came here. Don't feel sorry for us, Mack. There's a dope racket in this county. Willy and I talked it over and we want that racket stopped."

"Do you know anyone else who feels the same?" I asked.

Willy said, "I know two ex-marines with families. They'll do what I do."

"I can handle a gun," Wanda added.

"That's a start."

I went into the bedroom and collected the .25 pocket automatic. In my car, I loaded the cylinder and made sure that the Luger was loaded. I drove off. I needed help. There were five of us, but we needed more men.

Words ran through my mind. *An old man. A weak man. And afraid. One mighty shove, understand? Topple him from the throne. Take over. One million dollars, tax free.* Words were no good. What was needed was action, the big push.

In Midwood, 498 Maple Street proved to be a middle-class house with a starved-looking lawn and ragged shrubbery. The porch light was on. I rang the bell and Jake Tibbs answered in shirt sleeves. "Hello, Barry," he drawled, as if I had been expected.

We went into a side room, where Tibbs shut off television. His blue eyes were friendly as we sat down. "I heard some of the rumors and I get around. You're in trouble, neck-deep, I hear, but the details don't leak out yet. What's on your mind?"

"Sheriff, you get around in that old Ford, but you don't see all the dives." I lit a cigarette. "This is big, but it can be broken. And it has to be broken, and fast."

Step by step, fact by fact, slowly and meticulously, I went back over all I knew, dotting the *i*'s and crossing the *t*'s so he couldn't miss it. His blue eyes were steady on mine. Not once did Tibbs bother to interrupt with a question. My cigarette was long cold when I had finished.

"Well," Tibbs admitted cautiously, "I've heard some of this stuff. A little here, a little there. I didn't put it together the way you did, but you can do things a sheriff can't do. *You* can break the law. Maybe I should fit you for a cell. Barry, I'm only the sheriff. It's not my job to clamp down on the criminal element. I serve warrants and dispossess notices and foreclosures, all *civil* instruments, and that's the job of a sheriff. I'd like to help you, but—" Tibbs gestured helplessly.

I hated this man's willingness to shrug the whole thing aside. I had been right in my original diagnosis of him—smart, but timid. "In Jersey," I began persuasively, "isn't the sheriff the highest law officer in the county?"

"You're talking about the past, Barry. Laws stay the same, but men twist the law. Little by little, the sheriff has lost his power. The prosecutor is head man. He and his detective bureau supersede me. Law enforcement is too big for one man, like the sheriff. Did you talk to Frank Crews?"

"I came to you, not Frank Crews. In this setup, with Steady Eddy Flynn working with Parente, Crews can't help. You say you have no power today. Do you understand what a state of emergency is?"

"I'll listen."

"Whenever disaster strikes, a state of emergency exists. There's a powder plant outside Grove City—suppose it went up with a county-wide bang. Who'd be the emergency boss in that disaster?"

"I would, I guess."

"You *would*, and no guesswork. You'd even control any military unit which was called in. You'd take charge of all police and the detective bureau, if necessary. Why? The law still says a sheriff is the highest law enforcement officer in a Jersey county. Let's suppose that on a windy day, Midwood was swept by a fire, the life of the city menaced, business property threatened by looters. You'd take over, wouldn't you? You'd deputize as many men as you needed to control the situation. You'd command every police department in every town. Or, an A bomb might level Grove City. Maybe another type of emergency—say a labor riot and—"

Tibbs drawled, "We got the best volunteer fire department at Midwood. In Jersey, that is. Those boys could handle any fire without me. No A bomb is gonna explode. The last flood we had, and that *was* an emergency, was in '09. We've had no labor trouble, no race riot, no other big trouble in this county, ever."

"You have big trouble, now. This dope racket is a state of emergency, sheriff. If you saw the cellar of Helldorado, you wouldn't just sit there. Local people buy reefers in that cellar. I saw young girls there, headed for a living death. And Helldorado isn't the only spot where teenagers can buy reefers and heroin either. Pushers work everywhere. Pushers give the stuff to kids and hook them into a steady trade. Look what happened to poor Sherry Dalgren. The dope situation *demands* that you declare a state of emergency and take over. You must supersede Frank Crews and his crooked detective bureau. You've got to protect every home and every teenager in this county. If you wipe out this dope racket, and you can, sheriff, every decent citizen, every mother and father will pin stars on your chest that will last a lifetime, believe me."

Tibbs mulled over it. Finally, "Well, it's an idea. Sounds pretty big and dangerous to an average man like me. I mean, *me* taking over. I think this state of emergency thing is illegal—me grabbing the county and all the police and all the power. It might make me into a sort of Hitler, taking the government from the people. I can't do *that*. It just ain't legal." Tibbs turned to me. "Besides, I know Dominic Parente. He's not a bad sort. Haven't seen him lately, but he's not a bad sort. His rackets have always been in bounds—horse playing, numbers, craps, and maybe even women, but not enough to hurt anybody who can't afford to be hurt, unless it's somebody who insists on being hurt, law or no law. Barry, it's only been in the last few months that dope got in. Helldorado is new. It won't last. People won't stick to dope, see?"

Tibbs checked a pocket watch. "Ummm, after ten o'clock and she ain't in." He pocketed the watch. "Why don't you go to the governor, Barry? Hey, that's a good idea. Lay this in the lap of the governor, Barry."

I lit another cigarette and started on another tack. "Maybe you just lack the guts to do the job, sheriff. You've gots lots of company. You aren't the first sheriff to hold office and close his eyes to a mob."

Outside, a car braked suddenly, and Tibbs cocked an ear toward the street. "There's nothing remotely connected with a state of emergency here."

Tibbs looked toward the front windows. Outside, a car door slammed. When a hotrod gunned off, I tried to yank the sheriff back to the importance of what I was saying. "You must understand that the dope habit is a deadly disease, like cancer. It feeds on a person's vitals, and it can destroy a community. Dope is an enemy, sheriff, constantly at work and—"

The screen door had opened quietly, and Tibbs called, "That you, Margaret Ann?"

There was a moment of silence in the hallway, then a cool, young voice said, "I'm home."

"It's after ten o'clock, Margaret Ann."

"Oh, Billy and I were only goofing around."

"I want you to meet a friend."

"Do I have to?" Her voice took on a keen edge. "I'm tired tonight, daddy."

"Only take you a minute." Tibbs whispered to me, "I want you to meet my daughter," his eyes glowing with parental pride.

A cute young girl walked into the side room and blinked at the light. "I'm really tired." She had dark curls and her father's blue eyes, but the sleepy face was all her own. The loose sweater failed to hide the swelling signs of womanhood. "Billy had a record player in the hotrod and some new platters." She wore a plaid, knee-length skirt, ankle socks and scuffed saddle shoes. One elbow pinned a pocketbook against her side.

"Mr. Barry," Tibbs announced, "meet my daughter."

I said, "Hello, Margaret Ann."

The girl eyed the rug. "Hello."

"Margaret Ann is only sixteen," Tibbs explained, "and she's the president of the junor class in high. Last year she was the top student in the school and—"

The girl said sharply, "I don't *ever* want to hear that old routine again."

"But I only wanted to tell Mr. Barry how good you were."

The girl pounced on one word that her father had used. *"Were?* You mean *are!"*

"How good you are, Margaret Ann."

"Sometimes you sound like a square."

"Now, now," Tibbs soothed. "I'm only explaining to Mr. Barry. He's a detective."

Her blue eyes flashed up at me, then lowered defensively. The toe of one saddle shoe worried the rug. "I don't *want* you to explain me to anybody *ever*. For heaven's sake, why can't I go to bed? If you want to talk, talk all night, why do *I* have to listen?"

"I was only—"

"I suppose you'll tell this *perfect stranger* that I stay out too late. Just as if you didn't want me to have any *nice boy friends*, like Billy!" She still eyed the rug. In the obvious embarrassment of this family situation, I minded my own business. "All we did was goof around in the hotrod and listen to hot jazz. If you don't *believe* that was what we did, you can hire a detective to—to—" She jerked to a stop. Then, in the space of ten seconds, she seemed to withdraw deep within herself. When she spoke again, her voice had the cold remoteness of the stars. "I don't see why you always have to pick on me."

"Margaret Ann, I'm not picking on you."

"May I go to bed?"

"Of course."

The girl drawled, "You're a *detective*, Mr. Barry?"

"Sort of," I said.

"What kind of a detective?"

"Private."

Blue eyes flashed up for an instant. "Like in the movies and TV, Mr. Barry?"

"Hardly that romantic."

"Are you working on a case in town?"

"Unh, unh."

Lazily, the girl drifted across the rug. She offered me a hand, and her fingers were hot and moist to the touch. Her chin lifted and the blue eyes were almost frank. "It was nice meeting such a *handsome* detective." Her fingers exerted the slightest pressure. She stood there, just a cute kid, looking me up and down, the way kids will when they are interested in someone. "I hope we meet again, and soon, Mr. Barry." Her fingers squeezed. She stood there, no longer just a cute kid. There was a wanton invitation in the blue eyes. She pulled my hand to the right, turning my shoulder in toward her, then as she twisted toward her father, one burgeoning breast rubbed against my bare elbow. "I'm glad you introduced me to Mr. Barry, daddy." Her fingers were strong. One hip brushed against me. The fingers and hip said she liked me and would I see her again when the father was not around.

I pulled my hand loose and blushed to the roots of my hair. Her father, within two yards of us, was so immersed in fatherly pride that he missed the sexy play. I wondered how unobserving a man could be, until I remembered he was a father and thought of her as a child just beyond the doll stage.

Don't misunderstand me. I'm not that attractive to young kids. There was an explanation for what the girl had done. Right here in this bright room, with two adults watching, Margaret Ann was *stoned*. She had been smoking reefers. She had the tell-tale red-rimmed eyes and the tattling bodily languor, and if I had said suddenly, "Let's run off and ride the monkey's back," or, "Let's swing on the moon," or something equally stupid, she would have giggled uncontrollably. She was a mere kid in her own home, under the eyes of her father, and she was as full of sex as Ruth Crews. If you smoke up a joint, hit the weed hard, take off on a binge, you have no more morality than a common toad, no matter how old you are or what your upbringing has been.

Intuitively, I did something to turn this unbelievable development to my advantage. I jerked the pocketbook from under her elbow, and clicking off the latch, held the pocket- book upside down over a side table.

Margaret Ann gasped in alarm, "No, no," and tugged at my arm.

Tibbs began stiffly, "Barry, you have no right to—"

Of course, I had no right to grab that pocketbook. But it was a hunch, and it was too late to retreat. The contents cascaded to the table. Lipstick and compact. Folded handkerchief and tissues. Small change, two sticks of gum and a white comb. A boy's school ring, packets of folder matches, a memo book, a gold football. Lifesavers and a pencil. All the junk, all the necessities a teenage girl wads into a pocket- book, spilled there on the table. And something else, something that no teenager should ever possess—a careless length of wax paper, and peeping out from the loose paper, the tips of two brown cigarettes.

The girl groaned.

Her face was ghost-white, except for a red spot in the center of each cheek. Her mouth worked loosely as she struggled for words that would not come. She stood rooted to the rug, her arms like sticks, the fingers splayed. Suddenly, her eyes rolled wildly toward the ceiling. Then, she did what most kids do when they're caught—she fled. We heard her stumbling, frenzied dash up the flight of stairs, the opening and closing of a door. Then the silence was complete in the house rent only momentarily by the small sound of a key turning in the lock of Margaret Ann's bedroom door.

For a long moment, nothing stirred. Jake Tibbs took two slow steps toward the table. His fingers trembled as he touched the wax paper. Two reefers rolled out. He was a sheriff and he knew what they were. He sat next to the table and stared in disbelief. In the split second of realization of what his daughter had been doing with Billy, the road they had traveled to the music of hot jazz in that hotrod, what they had been doing other nights together, Tibbs had aged years.

And for myself, I wished that I had never entered this home, seen his daughter, recognized the obvious symptoms of the stoned, or dared rip the mask off this teenage victim of the vicious dope racket in this county. If I had not acted intuitively in grabbing her pocketbook, but had *thought*, I'd never have exposed her shame to her father.

Yet, thinking back, I wonder how else I could have forced Jake Tibbs to act to the fullest extent of his powers as sheriff?

To Jake Tibbs, and to a lot of parents, the dope racket is always somewhere else. It's over at the exereme edge of the county, among the illiterates; it's in some plush Helldorado where the idle wealthy seek exotic divertissement, it's up some dark alley in another town, in dark spots that we know exist, but which never touch us. Such a menace, even though we acknowledge it, has no more substance to us than a shadow. To shock us into a realization of the danger, the racket must come into our own home, into the familiar room where we sit. To force us into fighting back, we have to hold the evidence in our hands, like Jake Tibbs did there in his chair. And, if we need any further spur, we must listen to the weeping of a broken young girl in a dark bedroom overhead.

Presently, while Jake Tibbs sat there and shredded those cigarettes, I said quietly, "We must be understanding with young people. They always have too much eagerness and curiosity. With them, the question of morals is only soft wax, to be molded into habit. They reach for everything avidly, they try everything, they taste everything. They don't always recognize danger. We have to share the blame if anything goes wrong. I didn't come here to pry, Mr. Tibbs, and I should never have exposed your daughter. But maybe I can help. Would you tell me how long ago you noticed your daughter losing weight, Mr. Tibbs?"

I thought he had not heard the question. Then his lips moved. Words stumbled out. "Three-four weeks. Fourteen pounds, she lost. We worried, but she said something about a diet."

"At the table, during regular meals, did she eat well?"

"Always cleaned her plate."

Besides the training of a detective you ought to have the touch of a ministering saint to question a father in this situation. "Did she eat a lot of sweets, seem overly fond of sweets, particularly between meals?"

"Come to think of it, she did." He seemed to be discussing someone else, not his daughter. This was his momentary salvation. "Always at the cookie jar and into cake, my wife said. One day, she ate a quart of vanilla ice cream." His fingers worked ceaselessly on the marijuana. "Billy lives on the next street, the one behind Maple. I've known his father since before Billy was born, sixteen years ago. Billy is basketball captain next—next year."

"Has she exhibited red-rimmed eyes before?"

"Well, once or twice we noticed that."

"A runny nose?"

"That, too."

"An unexplainable cold, suddenly here, and just as suddenly gone again?"

"Now that you mention it, yes. Once or twice."

"When did you become aware of these symptoms first?"

"Let's see, oh I guess three weeks—well, four weeks back. About the time we thought she was losing weight."

"There's another angle, Mr. Tibbs. We must remember that those cigarettes cost a minimum of fifty cents each. During a panic—that's when police pressure is on—they retail for as much as two dollars. During the past three-four weeks, did she ask for more money than her normal allowance?"

"No."

"Did she ever do any work for pay, like baby-sitting?"

"No."

"Has any money been missing—household money you keep around?"

"No."

"I'm trying to understand and interpret *her* problem, Mr. Tibbs. I think we can fix the time of the first experimental cigarette about six or seven weeks ago. If that's true, and not more than one cigarette was smoked per day, the habit shouldn't be ingrained. She can be cured. She has extreme youth on her side, and that's a valuable ally. I know she can break the habit, and Billy can, too."

The last bit of marijuana had been reduced to powder. Jake Tibbs folded the wax paper meticulously around the stuff. "A reminder, is all," he said as he slid the paper into a pants pocket. "It better not be too late." He said it casually, but his drawn face was as rigid as wood. "She's about all we've got, I guess. I remember, she had croup once and we almost lost her. Couldn't sleep at all, for the worry. We pulled her through that. She's had measles and mumps, and she give us a scare once with a cold and aches. That was four years ago, in August, and we was worried about polio. Billy seemed to get whatever she got and maybe that was because they was always together. They was born in the same week and—"

I jerked away.

I can stand a woman's tears. But when a man weeps openly I want to go find a brick wall and tear it apart with my bare hands. You read of a thousand kids and adults who stumble down the marijuana road to a subterranean hell of heroin, nembutal, or cocaine, but if they're not part of you, the staggering numbers fail to shock you the way *one* case you can see, like Margaret Ann's, numbs you with impotent rage.

I did not turn to Jake Tibbs, until he said quietly, "It's all right, Barry. This is something neither of us figured. It's more of a state of emergency than I realized. Tell me exactly what's on your mind."

I sat down near him and began to talk. Step by step I outlined the plan I'd been building. I went over the things that I believed we had to do to get into position for the one hard blow at the core of the rackets empire in this county. He listened to the master plan, which stressed the necessity for secrecy and speed. Since he knew the county and the physical setup better than I did, Jake Tibbs suggested changes in detail, convincing me that he was smart and that his timidity had given way to strong purpose. When we had finished, it was Jake Tibbs who set the time and place for us to meet tomorrow morning.

We did not shake hands, nor did he accompany me to the door. I went out and down the steps into the deceptive serenity of this middle-class neighborhood. If this shocking tragedy broke wide open tomorrow, the town would be shaken to its roots. Billy, and Margaret Ann, and Sherry Dalgren, and who could say how many other teenagers? I felt like the fiend who has shattered a father's only dream, and as I drove off, knowing that the end justified the means didn't cheer me up.

I tiptoed into Willy Pickle's bungalow, making no noise, but Willy was awake. As I passed his half-open bedroom door, he said, "You in one piece, pal?"

"I was in no danger. All I did was load my guns, in case."

"In case of what?"

"We use the guns tomorrow night, Willy."

"That ain't soon enough to suit me," Willy grumbled, and closed the bedroom door.

It wasn't soon enough to suit me, either, but you can't implement a war in fifteen minutes.

CHAPTER ELEVEN

H IGH overhead the tiny stars stretched across the sky to infinity, but here under the interlaced branches of the tall trees it was very dark and very quiet, the only sound that of brook music off to the right. I wore a dark coat and trousers and a new hat with the brim pulled low to hide the whiteness of my face. My shoulder rig was heavy with the Luger, but the .25 automatic was a feather in one coat pocket. I figured that nobody, even in this bucolic stillness could possibly hear the whisper of my sneakers in the soft dirt of the ditch.

A couple of tree toads piped, and a few feet into the woods, some wild animal padded off with a rustle of dried leaves. A hundred yards away a car turned into the lane and headlights swung in a giant arc through the trees. I scrambled out of the ditch, stood against a tree trunk and waited. A sleek sedan tooled slowly past, its headlights flooding the thick shrubbery, the two fieldstone pillars and the closed gate with a sign that warned: CLOSED TO ALL THOROUGHFARE, etc. Forty feet away, as the sedan waited, a man parted the shrubbery. The discreet politician who guarded this first gate to Helldorado came over and leaned against the sedan.

Protected by the sound of the sedan's engine, I crept in an arc through the woods and slipped into the shrubbery. I met a chest-high stone wall. Toward the nearer pillar and behind the wall, loomed the roof of a structure the size and shape of a sentry box.

When the politician okayed the sedan, he passed through a door in the wall and clumped into the sentry box. His voice drawled casually, "Two in the next car, Ned. New Buick sedan." Something clicked, and I figured he had used a private telephone. The gate creaked open.

"Switch to low beam, please," the politician called politely. "Drive slow, Mr. Longwood."

I wonder how many times this lackey had issued that passport into hell. This was the next to the last time, I decided.

The purr of the Buick faded, and the gate creaked shut. On my watch the hour hand was glued to ten and the minute hand closed on twelve. The master plan against Dominic Parente's empire was in full swing.

A couple of tree toads resumed their piping. The politician lit a cigarette and the smoke drifted over the stone wall. Several minutes crawled by like centipedes, then a second car rolled to a stop by the gate. The politician strolled out. While he was gone, I slipped through the pedestrian's gate and peered into the sentry box. I could see nothing in the darkness, but taking a chance, I felt around and located a telephone. I hid on the far side of the little house.

The politician clumped into the sentry box and chattered over the phone. "Ned, this guy was here last night with two women. He must be feeling the bite because he's got only one woman tonight. An old Ford convertible with a valve tap."

The click of a replaced phone. The creak of the gate opening. I rammed the muzzle of the heavy Luger into his soft belly.

"Police," I warned. "This is a gun. Don't make a sound and don't reach for a button or this gun goes bang, understand?"

Breath wheezed from his body and he bleated, "Look, all I do is tend the gate and pass the word along."

"Who's Ned?"

"At the next gate, but I only—"

"Does Ned phone the building when a car goes through?"

"Yes, and I only—"

"You only tend the gate. Are there guards outside the building?"

"No."

"Can the inside guards see all of the parking lot?"

"Only if they light the floods. I gotta get the hell outa here! Look, I'm a county committeeman!"

"Step outside."

I backed up and he stepped outside. "Turn around." He turned around. He had all night; I was pressed for time.

If the Ford convertible failed to reach the second gate pretty soon, Ned might wonder where it was and phone here. This guard was only a county committeeman working for a dirty buck. I rapped him behind one ear with the butt of the Luger, not too hard. His big soft body spilled to the ground.

I crashed through the shrubbery, and Willy Pickle craned out of the convertible. "You knock him off, pal?"

"Yeah. Switch to dimmers."

Another car, without headlights, following the meshed seconds of the master plan, eased to a stop, and Jake Tibbs called out softly, "What about it, Barry?"

"He's only a county committeeman, and I handled him gently. Drop off a guard."

"Right."

Other dark cars, filled with raiders, piled up behind Jake's car. I climbed into the rear of the convertible and hid on the floor. The convertible moved off, and Wanda said, "There's no hurry, Willy," sounding bored. "How we doing, Mack?"

"Right on schedule."

Presently, the convertible stopped. Willy and the second politician, the one named Ned, went through the Longwood, Asbury Park, 219 Court Street routine, which we used to enter the grounds, and went back to his post. When Wanda fingered my neck, that meant the gate had started to open. I grabbed the left-hand door handle and eased the oiled door open. The convertible inched forward. When Willy stalled the engine, the car stopped between the pillars so the second gate could not close, and I was on the road with the convertible between me and Ned.

"Now what could have happened to the motor?" Willy wondered in a loud voice.

Ned returned to the road to ask solicitously, "Do you suppose you just stalled, Mr. Longwood, or could you be out of gas?"

"Either that or somethin' else."

"I suppose we'd better push the car off on the shoulder so as not to block the road, Mr. Longwood. If you'll give me a hand, then I can phone in for some gas and—"

I jumped at Ned from the side and jammed the Luger muzzle into his floating ribs. "Police," I warned.

Either Ned was a lot tougher than the county committeeman or younger and more careless with his life. Maybe simply more scared. Ned pivoted away from the Luger. I swung the barrel at the back of his neck and missed by inches. Ned took off like a jack rabbit and I chased him into a tangle of bushes. Rose thorns snagged my pants and bit at my face. I decided it was silly to follow Ned, and he crashed off through the woods without me.

I raced to the convertible. "We've got to move fast, damn it. He may meet another guard or pull an alarm." I swung aboard, the engine roared and the convertible gunned off.

Wanda said calmly, "Switch off the lights, you big lug. Slow down."

I glanced back. The next car passed through the gate without stopping. It seemed an eternity to the end of the white line on the road, and I had the door open before Willy parked under the spaced trees. Other cars drew up on the shoulder of the road. Shadows tumbled out and fell into groups.

"Let's go, Wanda," I whispered, and Willy chuckled.

"You kiss him real nice," he said.

"Tell Jake to hurry," I ordered, and taking Wanda's arm, strolled across the parking lot. Business was good at Helldorado. When the baby spot impaled us, we stopped. I wrapped an arm around Wanda's waist, and she turned to me on tiptoes, her back to the building. I kissed her lingeringly. This was business, and we had practiced the maneuver several times in Willy's kitchen, but without the kiss.

The low brim of my hat shielded my eyes from the spotlight, and I scanned the back wall of Helldorado. I saw something I had missed before—about the height of a second-story window, there was a small rectangle of glass. Of to the right, hugging the rear wall, shadows were creeping up. I broke off the kiss.

The guard upstairs must have been convinced we were just passionate lovers because the rear door swung open. We stepped into the dimly lit, square anteroom and paused by the sill. Wanda wheeled and clung to me. I had my back at the dorway. Just before the door closed, I slipped a thin piece of tin over the lock.

"Nice timing," I whispered, and Wanda smiled.

Leisurely, we crossed the anteroom to the inner door. Wanda jabbed a screwdriver into the space between the door and jamb. With both doors jammed, no suspicious guard could seal us in the anteroom.

"I hope somebody tries to close *this* door," Wanda whispered, giggling. The pearl-handled .32 filled her right hand.

I went back to the outer door and pushed. The door stuck. I backed off two steps, lowered a shoulder and plunged. My shoulder hit the door alongside the protruding tin, and the door exploded open.

Outside, the situation had changed—there must have been an alarm. Floodlights had turned the parking lot into noon. Something creaked overhead, and I glanced up. The rectangle of glass swung out. A man's dark face appeared for an instant, then vanished. He must have flipped a switch, because the door began to close. The Luger was inside my shoulder rig, but I had the automatic ready in my right hand. I braced one leg against the movement of the door and it stopped. Up there, a gun pushed from the window, then a hand, an arm and a face. As the muzzle lowered toward me, I snapped two shots with the .25. The man screamed, and the gun fell from his hand. The door started closing again, pinning me against the jamb.

"Jake!" I called.

Jake rushed up and tugged while I pushed, but the heavy steel door didn't budge. Two uniformed troopers added their strength, but the door still pinned me fast. One of the troopers grunted, "Get to work, Mike."

One of the troopers wrenched at the door with a crowbar. "Good thing you did get mixed up with this door, or the rest of us would probably be locked outside now," said Jake. "Where's Wanda?"

Wanda appeared from inside. "What are you waiting for, Mack?"

I thought it was pretty obvious. The damned door was mashing my chest. "Don't let anybody come through your door!" said Wanda.

"Don't worry!"

Someone grunted, "All together."

There was the tearing sound of metal, the door broke from one hinge, and the air rushed back into my chest as the men yanked the door aside. I leaned numbly against the jamb, and Jake Tibbs strode past, a gun ready. "You get back to the car and wait," I ordered Wanda.

A strident bell rang inside.

Wanda said, "Can't I see the fun?"

"Fun!"

Tibbs warned, "Get down, down!"

I pushed Wanda against the side wall, turned and saw Jake Tibbs fire. "Got one," Tibbs announced calmly, and I shoved Wanda toward the rear exit.

Suddenly, Steady Eddy Flynn yelled, "Hey, Tibbs! What the hell *you* doin' here?"

"A raid," the sheriff warned.

"You double-crossin' rat!"

Midway along the inside corridor stood Jake Tibbs. Steady Eddy guarded the narrow room beyond. I unlimbered the .25 and Tibbs roared, "Stand aside, you crooked cop!"

Both men fired, almost simultaneously. As I ran forward into the acrid smoke, I saw Steady Eddy pitch forward. I reached Jake Tibbs. "He get you, sheriff?"

"No, no. That's the end of Eddy, I guess."

Above the insistent ringing of the alarm bell, Jake bellowed, "Let's get on with it! Step over Eddy, boys."

We swarmed into the reception room. Guests streamed from the gambling rooms downstairs and Jake hollered, "This is a raid! Get back inside and you don't get hurt!"

A woman screamed. A man ran up to a brawny trooper and whined, "I gotta get home!" When in his anxiety to get out he clawed at the trooper's face, the trooper knocked him sprawling.

I moved toward the closed cellar door. Over by the lighted counter, a deputy smashed a crowbar against the glass shattering it into a thousand shards. There stood a middle- aged woman, her face the color of dough. "Don't shoot, don't shoot!" she screamed.

I wrenched the handle of the cellar door and it opened. The sound of hot jazz floated up the carpeted stairs. At my back Willy Pickle growled, "Let's join the party. You see Eddy, pal?"

"He's dead."

Willy had the Garand. "Yeah? And I figured Eddy belonged to me. Ready?"

There was a man in shorts at the foot of the stairway. He turned and staggered off. I glanced back, and beyond Willy were several troopers and two of Jake's deputies—the cellar detail. We ran down the stairs. The door of Number 6 opened and a wild-eyed woman stared out. She withdrew, like a turtle popping into its shell, and the door slammed.

A deputy ran forward and rapped on the door with a billy. "This is a raid, lady. I hope that's your husband in there."

I ordered, "One deputy take the stairs. Willy, you stay with me. The rest fan out and calm down the guests."

Before we could move, a young blonde bolted out into the corridor. She wore a mask and a diaphanous gown, and she carried a tray. She stopped as if she'd been slugged, and I recognized her as the empty tray clattered to the floor.

Somebody said, "Hey, she ain't wearin' a thing," and one of the troopers drawled, "With a chassis like that, she doesn't *need* to wear anything."

I grabbed the usherette's arm. A skinny man in his underwear drifted up, his eyes dreamy, and Willy yapped, "Hey, where you goin', bud?"

"He's stoned," I warned, and Willy turned the skinny man around and started him back along the corridor.

"Remember me?" I asked the blonde. "You said to come back, and here I am."

She began to scream, "Let me go, let me go," like a broken record, and I slapped her hard across the mouth. That stopped the screams and she sobbed, "I only work here, I only work here."

"Shut up or I'll slap you again, sweetheart," I said.

Along the corridor more doors opened and more puzzled faces appeared and disappeared. The troopers moved off and I could hear someone saying in a loud, calm voice, "This is police. Get ready for a long ride." Pause. "Hey, miss! You can't run around in your skin!"

Willy grumbled, "That's my marine friend."

I tore the mask off the blonde usherette. She was a scared kid. "What color eyes, kid?"

"G-g-green!"

"You're gorgeous, kid. Listen to me." My hand tightened on her wrist. "If you play nice, maybe I can let you off easy, understand?"

Willy chimed in with, "You oughta be home asleep. This rifle ain't for you. Where do they keep the junk?"

"Show us where they keep the junk," I ordered.

"If I—I do," she stammered, "you'll—"

"If you do, you won't go to jail," I promised.

She thought it over. "Okay. I'll show you. This way, captain."

I kept a firm grip on her elbow with the left hand, saving my right for the automatic. We hurried along the length of the corridor, turned a corner. Back here she chose one of a series of closed doors and said, "In here."

"I'll take it," big Willy said. He lifted a huge foot and kicked against a panel. The wood split, but the door held firm.

"It's unlocked," the blonde pointed out.

That didn't stop Willy. He set the Garand against the opposite wall, then barged across the corridor. One shoulder smashed the door open, and he sprawled into a lighted room. There was a white-jacketed attendant there, with a sap dangling from a cord around his wrist. I lifted the .25. Very carefully, the attendant let the cord slip over his wrist and the sap dropped to the floor.

"Don't move or I'll shoot," Willy thundered, scrambling to his feet. It sounded a little silly with no rifle in his hands, so he went out and came back with the Garand.

The attendant leaned his elbows on a mahogany bar flanked by rows and rows of liquor bottles. He drawled, "What's wrong with the guy lugging the Garand, eh?"

"He's bloodthirsty," I clipped off.

"Look, captain, I only work here, see?"

Willy shoved the muzzle of the Garand against the attendant's white jacket. "You better knock off work, bud."

He was a cool customer, that attendant. "Take that thing off my ribs. It tickles."

Any other time, any other place, it would have been funny. The blonde giggled anyway, and Willy glared and lowered the Garand. We were wasting time.

I asked the blonde, "Where do they keep the junk?"

"You don't know," the attendant drawled. "It's a state prison rap to *know* so you—"

Willy slapped the man, and the man fell in a heap, the words choking off inside his mouth.

"In there," the blonde said, pointing at a solid door at the end of the bar.

I crossed and tried the door. It had a combination lock. The blonde joined me. Her fingers were all thumbs on the lock, but she finally set the proper numbers and I yanked the door open.

It was a narrow, vault-like closet with a single lighted globe dangling at the end of a cord. There were shelves on both sides and to the right a white-jacketed attendant standing behind a tiny table. In one hand, he held a lighted match near a stack of boxes. "This is dynamite," he said quietly. "Do you want to see it go off?"

The blonde said, "The shelves on the left, captain."

"She's a rat," the man said. "You want I should blow up the joint, captain?"

Captain again. On a raid, you pick up commissions in a hurry. I waved the .25. "Drop the match." The match dropped harmlessly to the floor. "Step outside."

He grinned. "It wasn't dynamite, believe me. I was wonderin' if you scared easy." He strolled toward the bar.

Before a raid can be staged legally, it is necessary for someone to appear before a judge and attest to the fact specifically that such-and-such a law is being broken in such- and-such a place. Jake Tibbs had sworn before a judge this afternoon and obtained the necessary writ for our entry. All we needed to do now was produce evidence.

I turned to the shelves on the left and opened one of the boxes. It was packed full of panatellas. I tested three other boxes before I was satisfied there were enough panatellas to keep Helldorado in operation for a week of heavy trade.

Rows of cans, about quart size, stood on the bottom shelf. I worked the lid off one can and sniffed. It was filled with enough cured marijuana to roll fifty panatellas. Evidently the management employed an expert to roll reefers on the premises, but that could wait. There were more boxes and cans on the upper shelf and a small safe on the floor behind the table.

"What's in the safe?" I asked, and the blonde offered, "H—heroin caps."

"Do you know the combination?"

"No."

I pushed her out of the vault. The two white-jacketed men leaned indolently against the bar and the one Willy had slapped asked, "Do you want a slug of good Scotch, captain? It's on the house tonight."

I didn't want any Scotch. I wanted Tony Scales.

A trooper called from the doorway, "The sheriff wants to know if you located the junk."

"Yes. How's it going in the cellar?"

"They're getting dressed."

"How about upstairs?"

"They met two young punks who thought they were tough. One of them got it in the heart and the other's out cold. The trooper grinned. "They really have a setup here. The sheriff's having trouble getting into the second floor because the stairways are sealed off with steel doors. He sent back for a torch."

"Pass the word up to the sheriff that we've found the junk," I suggested. "Then come back and guard that door. The stuff's in there."

The trooper left, came right back, and grinned at the blonde. "Cute—all of her," he offered.

The blonde clamped both hands around my left wrist. "You said I could—" She tried to smile, but she was too scared for it to come out right. "Can I go, captain?"

"How long have you worked here?"

"A few weeks."

"Since the place opened?"

"Yes." She leaned hard against me and breathed, "Let me go, please."

"Know your way around this building?"

"If you mean upstairs—" She stopped.

The man who had been in the vault sneered, "She's gonna rat to the screws."

"You open that big mouth again and you'll spit teeth for a week," Willy growled.

"We'll go outside," I told the blonde, and Willy and I trailed her into the corridor.

Things had quieted down. Somebody had forgotten to shut off the music. A young deputy stood with his head inside a cubicle door, and we heard him say, "How can *you* get out of here, mister? Just like the rest—in the wagon." Pause. "What was that? Look, mister, you keep that hundred-dollar bill, for bail, or you go out feet first, on a stretcher!"

Willy said, "That's one of my marine buddies I fetched along. He's got a family, see?"

The marine went off with a fat man.

"What's your first name?" I asked the blonde.

"Ginny."

"Ginny, how do we get up to the second floor?"

"Captain, you promised if I showed you the junk, you'd let me go! I can get a long stretch for what I showed you! "

"Is there a way to the second floor from the cellar?" I questioned.

She shrugged, then brightened, saying, "Look, once we get up there, we can get outside. There's an emergency exit."

"Okay, you've got a minute to dress and you can make the emergency exit, kid."

Ginny scurried into a room and didn't bother to shut the door. Willy leaned the Garand against the wall. "I lug that thing in here an' don't even get a chance to shoot. What the hell kind of a raid is this, anyhow? Hey, you think this Ginny dame is on the level, huh?"

"It doesn't particularly matter. If she can get us upstairs, it will save time for the sheriff."

"She's stacked, and I mean *stacked.*"

"Remember Wanda, Willy."

"I ain't forgot about Wanda, but this Ginny draws the eye. How does a nice girl like her get mixed in this racket, huh?"

I didn't know, and said so. I didn't know how Wanda had gotten into the call girl racket, either, and I didn't care. I kept that to myself, but I did wonder if Willy would send Wanda on her way when he found out she had been a call girl.

Ginny hurried out, wearing clothes, and Willy commented, "I liked you the other way best."

"Which way do we go, kid?" I asked.

We trailed her into a storeroom, where she switched on a light. "I was always nosy," Ginny explained, flashing a confident smile. "I always arrived early to work and I used to snoop around. One night I discovered this."

It was a too-glib explanation. "This" was the open shaft of a dumbwaiter with the car waiting for customers. I helped Ginny aboard and crowded inside. Ginny said, "Willy, you close the door and push the top button."

Willy chuckled. "Have fun, folks."

The door closed and we sat in darkness. The elevator moved. Ginny's warm hand found mine. "Captain, the other night when you were here, I wasn't kidding when I asked you to come back and date me." She cuddled close. "I didn't expect it to turn out this way."

I let that drift into the darkness.

Ginny sighed. "If you had come back *alone*, we could have had a lot of fun."

"With reefers?"

"Unh, unh. I never smoked a joint, yet. *Real* fun, captain!"

"How old are you?" I growled.

"Nineteen, but I know what a handsome captain wants!"

"Local girl?"

"Carbondale." Her breast was pressed against my arm. "That's in Pennsylvania, and home was kinda dull." The elevator was a snail on vacation. "I went on my own at sixteen. Most of it's been fun, but you take the good with the bad. What the hell, I always say. I have my own apartment in Midwood."

The elevator stopped with a click.

"The Midwood Arms, captain. If you come—"

"How do we get out of this cage?"

She did something and a door popped open on a dimly lit corridor. All night it had been doors and corridors! There was a three-foot drop to the floor.

Jake Tibbs had told me something of this house. It was on the estate of an eccentric millionaire named Cotterby, who had built it in 1929, beating the Wall Street crash by a month. Cotterby had died during the last year of World War II, and his widow had had the place up for sale until Dominic Parente bought it two years ago. Parente had planned to live here, then decided to buy nearer Midwood.

I slid to the floor, turned. Ginny thrust her long, bare legs from the cage. They were lovely legs. She sat like that, a slow challenging smile spreading across her face. "Come see me sometime, captain, and we can—"

"Get the hell out of there," I snapped. "Behave, or I'll drop you downstairs and you can ride the wagon to jail."

She left the cage in a hurry. I said, "I want a snake named Tony Scales. Which way?"

"If he's here, he'll be in the office." Ginny slipped a hand inside my right arm. I said, "That's the gun arm," and she switched to the left arm. With her kind of rapid adaptation, she'd get along in a man's world. I had the .25 out, and snicking off the safety, remembered I had four bullets in the clip.

This narrow back corridor turned left, and we met a wide upstairs hallway lined with lighted wall lamps. "It's the last door on the right," Ginny said, "a corner room at the front. Tony wasn't nice-man at all. Always making passes at poor working girls. I hope he's there so you can beat his filthy brains to pulp!"

Nobody had to tell me what to do when I caught Tony Scales. "You go back to the dumb waiter and fetch Willy aloft." And I added, "Remember he's married."

"Husbands are the pushover type." Ginny drifted off. She was a likable kid, and her wiseness might be just a front.

I stalked the hallway, looking for trouble and finding only closed doors. At the last door on the right, I stopped and pressed my ear to the keyhole. Not a sound. I twisted the knob carefully—the door was unlocked.

I'm not any hero, even when I pretend to be. I flung the door inward and flattened against the side wall with my gun ready. Nothing happened. I counted to twenty, slowly, then peered around the jamb. Nobody said anything. I went in with the .25. The rats had fled leaving a single light burning at a huge desk.

This room was probably once the eccentric Cotterby's master bedroom. Now, its high walls were papered with hunting scenes, thick drapes covered two banks of windows, leather-padded chairs reminiscent of Parente's summer cabin in the hills were scattered around the room. Darkness filled the corners away from the desk. In the wall was a safe with the door ajar. The fat rats had escaped with the cash, too.

I crossed the thick rug and paused in front of the desk. It carried the usual accessories of business—spotlessly pure blue blotter, inkstand with *black* ink only, a fountain pen, an empty spindle, two telephones, and so on. In a hammered copper tray were four cigarette butts.

Two of the cigarettes had been smoked right down to somebody's lips. The other two butts interested me mainly because they were cork-tipped and were only half smoked. You can learn a lot about people from the cigarettes they leave behind. Idly, I picked up one of the longer butts. It wore a rouge smudge, a peculiar shade of dark red, almost the tinge of purple. Next to the cork was a delicate blue crown stamped on the white paper, and next to the crown, square blue lettering that formed the word, *Tareyton*. I dropped the butt on the tray because all it had told me was that it had been half smoked by a woman, a woman who used dark red lipstick.

I eyed the portable bar. On the shelf was a siphon, a silver bowl with three melted ice cubes floating in an inch of water, and a partially filled bottle of Teacher's Highland Cream, a good brand of Scotch. I sniffed the air, realizing there was a faint odor, perhaps of singed wool.

I started around the side of the desk and stopped in a hurry. Protruding from behind the desk were the soles of a man's black shoes. I had expected to find nobody in here. The man rested between the shoved-back swivel chair and the desk. He wore a two-hundred-buck suit and sported oily black hair. He was glossed-over hood, a guy named Tony Scales.

Tony didn't need any more young punks to guard him because Tony was headed for the morgue. He was no suicide, either. There was a bullet hole behind his left ear. The wound had bled surprisingly little, which meant that he had died very quickly. Powder burns pitted his flesh around the hole. An inch or so beyond the splayed fingers of Tony's left hand was a smooth length of cigarette ash. The story was trite. Somebody in Tony's confidence had stood behind the swivel chair, drawn a gun and fed Tony the big one. Tony had tumbled to the rug, and the lighted cigarette had slipped from his fingers and burned the deep wool rug.

I lowered to one knee and touched the ash. It was cold. I checked Tony's left wrist. There was no pulse, but the flesh was still warm. He had not been dead long. I figured back, checking against my watch. He had felt secure up here, in no hurry to leave when the raid started. Somebody had been with him or somebody had joined him after the noise of the alarm bell. Tony might have died ten minutes ago, or a little longer. From the size of the bullet hole, the gun was probably a .32. Anything bigger would have torn his head apart. The boys in ballistics could ascertain the calibre of the gun and possibly the make, too.

Beat his filthy brains out, Ginny had said. *He's not nice- man.*

His lady friend might have knocked Tony off, figuring that he was at the end of his rope, and decamped with the cash from the wall safe. Or the lady friend might have been gone long before the raid, or left by the emergency exit when the raid started. It didn't seem probable that she would hang around and await developments. It's inherent in most women to run when trouble starts.

That opened up another angle. Suppose Dominic Parente had been in here with Tony or downstairs? Parente might have taken this way to seal Tony's lips and partially close the trail to himself. And there was always the possibility that the fat cat behind the rackets had been here. Steady Eddy Flynn had been downstairs, which proved how confident this gang was. All right, let's say the fat cat had been here on Saturday night because that was collection time. Tony, then, had known the identity of the fat cat, so when the raid broke, the fat cat had killed Tony to shut him up. It figured.

I straightened up behind the desk.

Across the room there was a slight movement, and I focused in that direction. While I had knelt behind the desk, somebody had opened a second door near one of the corners of the room. Within the dark doorway someone moved. I glimpsed a pair of trousered legs and above them a leveled arm. A gloved hand was aiming a gun right at Mack Barry. I dropped instinctively, and in that instant the gun roared. A bullet whistled across the top of the desk and spanged into the wallpaper.

Willy bellowed from the hallway, "Mack, you all right?"

"Stay out!" I yelled.

I might as well have warned the wind. Willy stormed into the office, the Garand ready, and Ginny a step in his wake. I jumped up, swung the .25 toward the corner and saw only the closed door.

"He shot at me from that doorway," I said. "Whoever he was, he killed Tony Scales. Tony's behind the desk."

"Dead, huh?" Willy grunted, and headed toward the door.

Ginny said, "Good! Not that you got shot at, captain, but that Tony is dead, good!"

"Locked! " Willy yelled, rattling the knob.

"But Tony always kept it unlocked," Ginny wailed. "Captain, that's the emergency exit. Now what do I do?"

I didn't care what she did. "Tell me about that emergency exit," I said, noticing the lipstick on Willy's face.

"It's the way Tony often came in and out. That way, nobody downstairs knew if he was up here or not, or out at the White Swan tending to that business."

"Important man, wasn't he?"

"Very important."

"Did Tony bring a girl friend in here, Ginny?"

"Which *one?*"

"How many did Tony have?"

"Two or three and they've always been in here, one time or another. Tony was a rat."

"How do you know so much about this place?"

"Well—"

She didn't have to tell me. She'd told enough lies. She hadn't snooped in this building because she had never had to snoop. She had been up here with Tony Scales often enough to know the setup.

"Did you always sneak upstairs in the dumbwaiter?" I sneered.

Ginny smiled brazenly. "Okay, so I knew Tony. He was my boss and who says no to the boss in a dump like this?"

"Where does that door lead to?"

"It's a stairway into the cellar, then a tunnel under the front lawn to the woods."

I bought that. Jake Tibbs had said that Cotterby, who built this place, was eccentric, and there very well might be tunnels and hidden staircases all over the place. *Why* Cotterby had had them didn't matter. "Ginny, can you get into the cellar proper by that stairway?"

"Certainly."

"Why did you bring me up in—hell, skip it."

I knew why we had used the dumbwaiter together, but if we had only used the stairway, I'd have caught the killer. He was a pretty cool customer, to loiter in leisure up here, then open that door for pot shots at me. "You're a bright, little tart," I said. "Can you get upstairs without the dumbwaiter or secret stairs?"

"If you have the combination to the steel doors, captain."

"Do you have the combo?"

"Unh, unh. And Tony didn't give me the combination to that wall safe that's open, either."

"Did Tony tell you who the fat cat is behind the rackets?"

"No."

"Okay, Willy. Shoot the lock off that door to the private stairway."

We all backed into the center of the room. Willy knelt and leveled the Garand. Before he could fire, the desk light went off and the lights in the upper hallway faded away.

"Just when I had a bead," Willy grumbled in the darkness. "Take my flashlight, pal."

I took the flash. "Ginny, do you know what happened?"

"There's a master switch by the first landing, on the way to the cellar. The bastard must have pulled it."

Whoever had shot at me had deep-freeze blood in his veins. I centered a beam on the lock. "Clip it, Willy."

Willy fired a clip. Empty shells bounced to the rug. Burned powder tickled our nostrils. Wood splintered around the door knob. I walked over and kicked the door open.

"None of your intuition," Willy warned. "That guy may be on the landing."

He wasn't on the landing. The flashlight showed a narrow, steep flight of stairs with a miscroscopic landing at the first floor. On the wall was an open hand switch that had been pulled. I had to use the handrail to negotiate the stairs and throw the switch.

I crept down a second flight of stairs, Ginny and Willy behind me, to a damp cellar room with two doors. One door opened into a dark tunnel, and I went through the other door into the cellar. I located a trooper and relayed a message to Jake Tibbs about the stairway to the second floor, where he could find Tony Scales, adding, "Willy and I are following a hot trail. Tell Jake not to worry."

"If I can find Jake. He's been hard to locate recently."

Inside the tiny room Ginny said, "You'd better watch your step in that tunnel, captain. There's a right angle turn. If that bastard who shot at you tries again, it'll be at the corner."

Using the flash and carrying the Luger, I entered the tunnel. It had a six foot concrete ceiling so that I had to stoop, side walls of cheap red brick, and then the eccentric Cotterby must have run out of money because the floor was only dirt. The long beam picked up the right angle turn.

I handed the flash to Willy and told him to focus into the corner. I balanced my hat on the Luger's barrel, and kneeling, inched the crown into the turn. The bastard was still around, cucumber cold. A pistol roared twice, and my hat flew off the Luger. That was damn good shooting. Pieces of broken brick peppered my face and red dust billowed in the flashlight beam. From the sharp sound of the pistol, I decided he used a .32, wondering if the accoustics of the tunnel had distorted the report.

"Lights out!" I yelled.

The beam died. I dropped into the outside corner, and prone on the dirt, sprayed three shots from the Luger. In this confinement, the Luger had the sound of a cannon. "Lights, Willy!"

Willy had the bit in his teeth. Disdainfully, he stepped around the corner and the long beam reached over me, out through the drifting smoke and dust to finger an open exit.

"He ran for it," Willy said calmly, and ran ahead.

I scrambled after Willy and the weaving beam. Ginny wailed, "Don't leave me!"

We burst from the exit and landed in the woods below the house. The beam picked out bushes, azaleas and rhododendrons. "Put that light out," I whispered, and Willy cut it.

As we waited, an engine started up near by with a roar. We crashed through the thick bushes toward the noise. A car gunned off. We plunged into a lane in the woods where the car had been parked. At the end of the lane, a black sedan left the woods and hit the white-lined road. We ran, and Willy gasped, "He can't get through the gates!"

As we reached the open, we saw that the first gate was shut. The black sedan simply cut across lawn, circling the gate, and lurched back onto the road. Willy knelt.

"Range a hundred fifty yards," I said.

The Garand began to speak. Willy spaced the shots. Two bullets kicked dirt behind the sedan and the third spanged into a rear fender. I think Willy would have stopped the sedan, but trees intervened. Willy finished the clip anyway.

"Lousy shootin'," he grumbled.

From down the road, out of sight, came a loud splintering sound of metal on wood, and Willy said, "I guess he didn't stop for that gate to open." Seconds later, and much too late, a .38 positive started to boom. Brakes shrilled in protest. A moment, and then headlights flicked on, and a car zoomed off down the macadam highway.

"He got away," Willie decided.

Our luck had run dry. Yet I sensed a developing pattern in this killer's action. He might be improvising but he was certainly cool in the crisis. "We may find a couple of knuckleheads," I decided, "at the White Swan."

A deputy ran up from the first gate. I asked, "Did you get a good look at him?"

"Only his hat."

Willy growled, "Should have used the BAR gun."

"Look, he went around that gate like a bat outa hell!"

"We'll be trailing him right out," I said. "Get back to the gate and don't let anybody else out."

The deputy went back to his post, and Ginny ran up. "I—I thought you two—ditched me! Did you plug the guy?"

Willy chuckled. "We went off like a bat outa hell. Pal, do you think I should load this Garand?"

"It's no good for close work. Come along, Ginny, and we'll take you out of here."

"Captain, I love you!"

We crossed the starlit lawn, passed the parked cars of the raiders, and met Wanda under the trees. She had the .32. "What was all the fuss out there?" she wanted to know, and I told her tersely. I don't think that Wanda was listening because she asked, "Who's the girl?"

"Ginny, the usherette," I explained. "She helped us inside and we're going to let her go free."

"Ginny, eh?" Wanda purred. "That's the one who had the body beautiful and wore the mask. And the cobweb gown."

"I'm tired," Ginny said. "Scratch some other face."

We walked to the convertible and I took the wheel. Willy said politely, "Ginny, I'll help you get in the back seat."

Wanda said sweetly, "She'll ride up front with Mack."

"That's kind of you," Ginny put in. "Willy, you're awfully sweet. I won't be too far from you." Ginny joined me and snuggled close.

The engine turned over with no coaxing. From the back, Wanda pointed out, "You didn't help *me* into the car."

"Maybe," Ginny suggested, "you should wear cobwebs."

"Hey, don't shine that flash in my face," Willy cried.

"Wipe the lipstick off your face," Wanda ordered.

Ginny giggled. "The trouble some women have holding a man." I drove off, hoping' the cats wouldn't scratch each other's eyes out.

The deputy opened the first gate and we went through. Further along, the second gate was open, half of it swinging crazily, the rest knocked to the shoulder. A trooper manned this exit and he held a .38 positive on us until he saw who it was.

"You see who drove that sedan?" I asked.

"I saw only a crazy man's hat with the brim low. I thought he was going to stop but he went through that gate like a bat outa hell."

"How's the county committeeman?"

"What?" The trooper laughed. "You mean the guard that's handcuffed. He threatened to pull his rank and have *me* arrested for *false arrest*. Hot up at Helldorado?"

"It was hot for a while."

I drove off. I drove fast, but it still took twelve minutes to reach the rear of the White Swan and park in the shadows. "Willy, listen carefully. You're to go in first. Don't notice me. When I start for upstairs, give me a thirty-second start, then you trail right up, understand?"

"Right. Do I fetch the Garand along?"

"Take my .25. This is no raid."

I reloaded the Luger with a spare clip, and Willy started off. "Take good care of yourself this time," Wanda warned, and Ginny twisted around on the seat and said in a saccharine voice, "We didn't really neck, Mrs. Willy. Only a few kisses."

I stepped from the car. Wanda stopped me long enough to snap, "Do I have to wait here with this naked usherette, Mack?"

"It won't be long."

"Did you leave the key in the ignition?"

"Yes."

I slouched off, and Ginny called, "Good luck, captain."

I stopped. It was time that I straightened her out. "I'm only a private investigator on a case."

"That's all right in my book, Mack. You'll always be a *captain* in my heart!"

Those were corny words, straight from a soap opera script, but sometimes I'm a sucker for corn. I carried my shoulders straighter on the way to the White Swan, and ignored Wanda's loud snickering.

CHAPTER TWELVE

INSIDE the Swan, patrons jammed the stools. Thirsty customers crowded two deep behind the stools, and the waiters had to use shoehorns to stuff more guests into the booths. Tonight there was the usual smoke and noise, but more men than women—progress in any barroom.

Willy lounged near the middle of the bar, swigging from a bottle of beer. Periodically he cleaned suds off his mouth with a swipe of one paw. He saw me and winked hugely.

I wormed among the customers, and heard a man say, "The sheriff kicked over Helldorado, Valerie."

"I wondered where Tony and his boys were," Valerie said. "A very nice man, Tony."

"You can say that again."

I maneuvered between two women perched on stools. The one to the right had a young hungry face, like a *Vogue* model, with half of her small, slim superstructure popping from a low-necked gown. Hungryface drawled, "Pahdon me for bumping you, mah lawd."

"You're pahdoned," I said.

The one to the left had a young plain face and good front lines, sheathed in a high-necked dress. Plainface smiled and offered, "Pardon me, but there's a smudge on your cheek, darling."

I said, "You're pardoned."

I fingered Mike, the bartender, and laid a sawbuck on the wet bar. "Whatever the ladies will have, and a double rye on ice for me." When the drinks arrived, Mike took the sawbuck and went off.

"I shan't drink it, you know," Hungryface drooled, and Plainface said, "Thank you, darling."

"What's your name?" I asked.

"Helen."

"I like girls named Helen."

"You go right on liking me, darling."

Mike returned with change. I leaned across the bar and buzzed his cauliflower ear. "Keep the change. Is Tony around?"

"No."

"Will he be in later?"

"No."

"Tony said to bring the stuff here. Who's around?"

"Go wet a duck's back," Mike grunted, and stalked off with the balance of my sawbuck.

Something soft rubbed against my left arm. It was Helen. She had moved close to me. Now she whispered, "Tony drew the big one tonight, darling."

"Too bad. Nice guy, Tony."

"Not nice-guy, Tony. You know this layout, darling?"

"Just the bar."

"If you're curious, you'll find the restrooms at the rear. You can't miss the stairway."

"Thanks."

"That's a big gun you wear, darling. Pete Castille was in, and I don't think he went out. Be careful, won't you?"

Hungryface butted into the conversation and drawled a dirty story filled with pungent words. I decided not to wash out her mouth and finished the rye.

Helen said, "I want you to come back, darling," and I hoped I would. I *did* like girls named Helen.

Willy had tapped a fresh bottle of beer, and he had a big wink for me as I passed. Some day, if I let him stick around, I'd have to teach him *my* business. I saw Ruth Crews in a crowded booth, but she didn't see me because she was too busy with a young, virile-looking sailor. At the back, I wandered into the corridor, where I found two restroom doors and a wide, unlit stairway with a velvet rope across the bottom.

There was nobody around, so I ducked under the rope and mounted the wide stairs to a middle landing. Up above me loomed the other half of the staircase, plenty of darkness, and a balustrade for the protection of stray drunks who might tumble into the stairwell otherwise. I was a couple of steps from the top landing when a shadow rose on the wall beside me, chopping down with one arm, and a sap exploded at the back of my head.

I pitched forward into blackness.

Somebody kept growling in my ear, "You drink all of this," and the same somebody tried to pour cold beer into my lungs. It was only Willy with an original brand of first aid treatment. He had propped me against the wall, and he seemd worried. "Pal, you was out cold on the top steps. You bump into somethin'?"

I didn't feel like briefing him on the fundamentals of my business just then. "I ran into a shadow with a sap."

"That guy we been trailin'?"

"Possibly." The lump at the back of my head was the size of a walnut. If the shadow had struck an inch lower, I'd be ready for the basket and a trip to the county's morgue. "Who came downstairs?"

"Nobody come down."

"Who went out the window?"

"I haven't checked that, pal."

"You came upstairs right after I did?"

"I just stopped to say hello to Ruth Crews and her sailor an' then I came right up."

I looked at my watch. It said that Willy had arrived five-six minutes too late to get himself sapped. "Willy, when this is over, I'm going to do you a favor."

"What?"

"Buy you another farm so you can stick to gardening. Let's see what they have up here."

One room took up half the floor. It was an office rigged with neon lights, air conditioning, sound proofing, steel- shuttered windows, an open safe that had been rifled, desks, tables, a dozen telephones, two spilled filing cabinets, and the rest of the equipment necessary in the operation of an efficient wire room. Pete Castille hadn't left. Willy found him behind the only big desk in the room, his face kissing the floor.

Pete Castille was the same dark, wide-shouldered muscle boy I'd met briefly at Dominic Parente's that first night. He wore one of my souvenirs—a broken nose, and somebody else's memento—a neat hole behind his left ear. He was a victim of the double-cross, suddenly popular in this county.

Willy said, "Dead, huh?"

"Dead."

"You think the bastard who got Tony Scales did this?"

"Yes. It fits a developing pattern."

"The same bastard who shot at you twice and sapped you on the stairs, right?"

"Step to the head of the class."

"Look, knockin' off his own pals don't make sense."

With plush Helldorado, the heart of the rackets smashed, it made sense. My watch warned that it was twelve o'clock, and I was going to arrive late for a certain Saturday night date with Biz Parente. "Willy, I'll give you a chance to be promoted. We know that Steady Eddy Flynn was the top cop in the rackets and Jake Tibbs killed him at Helldorado. Tony Scales was one of the top operators, and Tony's gone. Pete Castille was in the know, and Pete's finished. What have you got?"

"Three dead rats."

"But each rat is top drawer in the racket, and full of too much information. Some big shot, and I think it's the fat cat, is busy covering the trail to himself. If he kills Dominic Parente and his wife, the fat cat's home free. Who are we trailing?"

Willy scratched his moon face thoughtfully. "All along, I been kinda puzzled. Look, ever since Jake Tibbs killed Steady Eddy, Jake don't come around once to see what *we're* doin'."

"Pick up your diploma, Willy."

It had to be that way.

I dragged on a cigarette and mused. There wouldn't be much sense in Dominic Parente's knocking off his top lieutenants. Frank Crews was too soft for a killer's role. But Jake Tibbs was the perfect fat cat.

As sheriff, he was top enforcement officer in the county, and that's plenty of weight to fat-cat any racket. In the Helldorado, Steady Eddy had called Tibbs a double-crosser, and Steady Eddy knew his way around. Tibbs had murdered Steady Eddy. The raiding party had been organized meticulously into separate details, each with a leader, so that Tibbs could circulate freely. Not once had we seen Tibbs, since he entered Helldorado, and just before we left, a trooper had said, "I'll take your message to him, but he hasn't been around lately." Tibbs had been *too busy to be around.*

He had known about the secret passageway upstairs. He had gone up there and killed Tony Scales, shot twice at me, escaped in the sedan, driven here and finished off Pete Castille. In killing Steady Eddy, Tibbs had proved he was a crack shot with a gun, and only a crack shot could have winged my hat in the tunnel.

And Margaret Ann, Tibbs's daughter? It must have been a shock to discover that his own daughter had become a victim of one of the rackets he fostered. Perhaps Tibbs had organized the raid as a personal revenge. Or he had decided the rackets were doomed—Biz Parente had said it needed only one mighty shove—and Tibbs had pulled out, then busied himself with covering the trail.

The old Ford, the middle-class home, the shoddy clothes? The window dressing of false respectability. Tibbs was a smart rat, playing it close to the billfold, with the graft stashed in the all-too-familiar safe deposit box. He must have made a fortune as fat cat. I crushed out my cigarette.

"Willy, we'll stop in the men's room, then walk out as if we knew nothing, understand?"

"Right."

"You'd better not mention to Wanda that you talked to Ruth Crews for five minutes."

"They're friends."

"But just tonight don't mention any other woman to Wanda."

We sneaked downstairs unnoticed. I should have hurried, but I didn't. I washed up. If the Parentes were dead, they were dead from Jake Tibbs's gun. We walked out unhurriedly and found Wanda alone in the convertible.

"Where's Ginny?" I asked.

"Ginny went for a walk, Mack."

"Why?"

"I drove Ginny a mile toward Midwood," Wanda purred, "and dumped her by the road, and she went for a walk."

"She was tired," Willy said. "Why did you do that to poor Ginny?"

Sweetly, "Sit with me in the back seat, Willy, and I'll tell you why it was best for her to go off."

I manned the wheel. "Wanda, we're taking you home first, then Willy and I will go out to Parente's home, okay?"

"Don't you let Willy get hurt."

I started the engine. Wanda said, "Willy, did you collect any more lipstick?"

"No."

"Did you speak to any woman?"

"Uh—no."

"Did you, darling?"

"Hell, no," Willy said stoutly.

"I want you to listen carefully. You're a nice guy, something special in my book. I don't want anything ever to happen to you. You must realize there are a lot of loose women in this world and—"

I dialed out the lecture and drove toward Willy's bungalow. I knew a lot about women and I suppose that's the main reason why I'd never married. After a tough case I didn't want my brains picked by any inquisitive female.

It was long past midnight. In the soft spring night the stars looked as if they were floating ten feet up.

Parente's garage stood parallel to the house under an elm. We walked the lawn and sneaked inside the garage. There were four cars parked for the night—a Lincoln sedan, a Caddy convertible with leopard-skin seat covers, a blue Chrysler sedan and a Ford panel truck. We chose the Lincoln.

Both headlights were smashed, the front bumper twisted, the chromium grille stove in. If we needed any more evidence, gate splinters stuck in the grille and one fender wore a ragged hole from a Garand bullet.

"A county car," Willy whispered. "Like Jake could drive, only he uses that old Ford."

Jake hadn't used the old Ford tonight. I fingered the hood. The engine was still hot. "Jake's still around," I decided. "I'm going inside alone and see who's alive. You guard the garage."

"With the Garand?"

"Yes, and you'd better hand over that .25."

The Luger was in my shoulder rig, the .25 in my pocket. "If Jake makes a run for a car, don't ask any questions. Shoot first and we'll question the corpse. I want to get you home to Wanda in one piece. Have you got that straight?"

"Sure, *captain.*"

I worked toward the house. At the rear, light shone from the open doorway of the solarium. I went that way quietly, paused just off the patch of light on the lawn. Inside I saw the narrow table supporting the lamp with the opaque shade, the white rug, the lush plants in copper tubs, the claret cushions on tubular furniture, and the fan-backed chair with a familiar occupant.

A white sweater draped her upper body and a green skirt emphasized the rich fullness of her thighs, but her lower legs were bare. Her legs were crossed, displaying dimpled knees, and her eyes were closed. She was neither asleep nor dead because a fresh cigarette glowed in one dangling hand.

"May I come in, please?" I asked.

Her eyes opened, and she said, "Of course."

I crossed the virginal rug to her chair. Her black eyes were expressionless. "It's so late I thought you'd forgotten our date." She rubbed the cigarette out in a tray that held two long butts. "One never knows about men, does one?" She pouted but her eyes were still blank.

"Aren't you going to kiss me?" she asked.

I leaned down. She lifted her arms and clasped the back of my neck. Her lips, at first cool and inquisitive, grew warm and pliant. "My darling," she whispered, and stroked my face. "I thought you'd never, never come. I've been sitting here for hours, waiting for you."

"I couldn't forget you."

She was sheer loveliness, her body warm against me, her dark eyes shining now, cheeks glowing, and crimson lipstick so smooth on quivering lips it looked a part of her.

"What I like most about you, Biz, is your unpredictable character. You were two women at the lake yesterday, and now you're somebody else. You're a chameleon."

"Goodness, isn't that a—a lizard?"

"You're just like a chameleon. Let me show you."

I cupped her chin in one hand, then ran rude fingers through her black hair, rumpling the set of the curls. Her eyes smoldered and she growled through clenched teeth, "Don't do that again."

"I won't. The last time I played rough, you damn near killed me with the convertible, remember?"

"Save your toughness for men!" she snapped, sitting down quickly.

"Just like a chameleon."

"You bastard!" Slowly, the fire faded from her eyes, and she smiled. "All right, a chameleon. You teased me deliberately, but you didn't come here to tease me."

"No, to help you."

Biz took my hand and tried to pull me down to her. I pulled roughly away. There was danger inside this house and the feel of it nagged at my nerves.

"When we made this date," I told her, "nothing was said about love-making. You said I could topple a king from the rackets throne. Business first."

She was seething like the sea before a storm, yet she had far more control than Ruth Crews. She stood up, and standing wide-legged, circled my hips with strong arms and tightened the grip. "I'll never, never let you go!" Her eyes measured me. "Are you sure you wish to go through with this?"

"I came, didn't I?"

"I'm not forcing you against your will?"

"No."

"It's your choice?"

"My choice. You made it difficult to refuse. A million dollars in it, you said."

"If it's only for the money—" Her arms slackened. "I was right the first night about you. You'll take a woman, but it's going to be when *you* want to."

"Unh, unh. That wasn't true at the lake yesterday and it isn't true now. I like money, but I like a beautiful woman more than money, and you're a beautiful woman."

"I'll make you happy!"

"You have."

"Deliriously happy!"

"Business first. How do I topple him?"

Her arms slid up to my shoulders, and I knew she would discover the Luger. She did, and unbuttoning my coat, pulled out the gun. "Goodness, it's so heavy."

"It's part revolver and part automatic. The bullet can tear off a man's head."

"Really?"

I nodded.

The heavy Luger sagged in her hand and the muzzle rested on my chest. "Goodness, if this went off—" Her forefinger tightened ever so slightly around the trigger. "There, by your heart—it would tear out your heart, if your heart were black, wouldn't it?"

"Yes."

"Remember that, my darling."

"But first, you'd have to release the safety."

"Oh. I'm stupid about guns. Show me."

I showed her how to release the safety with a thumb, then holstered it, leaving the coat unbuttoned.

"You're not to kill him," she murmured. "You're strong and tough, and he knows that. Which should be enough. You can use a psychological approach because he's old and weak and afraid. He realizes that the setup has been slipping from his grip, and he doesn't know what to do to stay on top. So you must be the boss and hold him to the course we set. Poise a threat. If he does not do such-and-so or this-and-that, according to direction, *then* there's force. Perhaps a momentary show of force, like—"

"Don't tell me the business of thuggery."

"—slapping him around to prove who's the boss. He must not realize we have need for him. You're not to kill him, understand?"

"You don't have to draw blueprints."

"Since you're not going to kill him or use the gun to beat him, suppose you give me the Luger."

I handed over the gun, trying to remember if I had called it a Luger in her presence. She said softly, "You're awfully sure of me, aren't you?"

"No."

"I'm sure about you, my darling." She dropped the Luger carelessly on the side table. There was a tenseness in her movements and an emotion at work inside her that I couldn't place for the moment. "Tell me how you'll do it."

"Silk glove treatment. The way the racket boys work. No guns, no fists. The suggestion of guns and fists, *if*. The racket boys understand applied psychology. The threat of force is more blood chilling than the actual gun or the sickening thud of a fist. And always, I remember, this is the big deal. For a million dollars. For a beautiful woman."

"Show me."

I shrugged. "So you want to call it quits," I said, in the flat, hard monotone of the racket boys. "Look, we play by rules. Once we deal you in, you're in for keeps. There's only one road, no turning off, understand? Get something else straight in your mind. You *were* the big boy. No more. I'm taking over, understand? From here in, I give the orders. Nobody quits on the big boy. *If* you try a fast one, I know what to do. Only you're not going to rat out on *me*."

"That's when you slap him, big boy."

"Telling me my business again. Okay, so that's when I slap him, but easy. He's old and I don't want him to blow a fuse. Where the hell's the throne room or do you have to lead me around by the hand?"

"Turn right off the circular lobby. It's the first door right. He doesn't know you're coming."

"You set him up good?"

Her lips curled. "He's not only weak, he's drunk tonight. Go take him."

"Right."

"I'll wait here for you."

The new big boy went off to topple Sheriff Jake Tibbs from his fat-cat roll. Without radar, I located the correct door. Of course it was closed. All night I had been opening and closing doors, and I was getting fed up with it. I opened this one and didn't close it.

It was a spacious room with a high ceiling, but hardly a throne room. A man was slumped in a wing chair, his feet on a hassock and his shoes off. He was no king, the county supine at his feet, but a tired old man facing the indisputable barricade that marks the end of a one-way street. But, it was not quite time to settle him, and I returned to the solarium.

Biz waited in the fan-backed chair, and stopped sipping Scotch long enough to say, "Good heavens, you're a fast worker. He's in line already?"

"It's not going to be as easy as you thought it was. The fat cat will keep, but something else won't. I've been puzzled about one man, Biz. Not once have you mentioned your husband directly, not once has he shown around here. Where is he?"

She seemed to back into a shell. Setting the glass on the table, she said, "I thought you were a smart private detective. You've talked to a number of important people since you came to town. Don't *you* know where my husband is?"

"Rumor says he's not around."

"Of course not." Biz picked up a jeweled cigarette case. "When you weren't inquisitive about my husband, I thought you knew." She took out a long cigarette and closed the case. "He's been ill for some time. A light, please."

I used her jeweled lighter, which matched the case. I made a flame and steadied it. "Caddy convertibles, stone martens, and now jewel-studded gewgaws." She sucked smoke into her lungs. "You've got a pleasant life, with all the luxuries. What about your husband's illness?"

"You might as well know, because it lightens your task. Last August my husband had a serious nervous breakdown. For several months he was actually a little demented. Later, when he regained a modicum of sense, he was so exhausted that the doctors confined him to bed. This was all hush-hush, of course. Then, the doctors discovered that he had cancer. Since Thanksgiving, my husband has been confined secretly in a private sanatorium, alternately off his rocker and sane, but always in bed and incurably ill. It's simply a question of which day he dies."

She stopped talking and concentrated on the cigarette. When it was half smoked, she extinguished it meticulously alongside several butts with crimsoned cork tips. Then, casually, "In the sort of business my husband operated, a strong hand is required all the time. At first, there was a stop-gap arrangement with Pete Castille and Tony Scales sharing honors, but that didn't work because they were geared to lieutenancies, rather than the job of top executive. Also, if one were chosen as boss, the other might step out of line. The man in the other room knew this. When he was in charge, he had always stayed in the background, taking generous slices of ice and arranging the green lights whenever necessary.

"On Labor Day, he decided to take over the businesses completely. I was only a woman, inexperienced in business. Before I realized what had happened, he had *literally* taken over. Because of the—well, special nature of the business, he was able to acquire deeds to various properties, the actual businesses through corporate manipulation, and even dip into the cash reserves. As I understood from Tony and Pete, tremendous sums of cash must be readily available. They worried because it made their work doubly difficult, working on such narrow margins of cash. As for myself, I thought he was being unethical to take advantage of my poor husband's illness. Why, he even acquired the deed to this house and today, it's registered in his name! He could toss me out tomorrow, if he chose, which shows you my precarious position. Darling, I have only two servants at present, here only during the day, and one yard man and no chauffeur!"

"Tough," I said.

She leaned forward. "That's why I need a strong man with brains—someone like you—to replace my husband." Her fingers worked nervously with the hem of her skirt. "To make matters even worse, he got a grandiose idea and started a plush gambling club called Helldorado, which cost a hundred thousand dollars to open and which barely meets the payroll! Everyone in the organization is restless, so Tony and Pete say, and they are almost rebellious. I don't think he realized the magnitude of the operation until he was in too deep to withdraw. He seems so much older and weaker, so much more afraid. It was fortunate for me you arrived at this crucial moment. When I first met you, I was impressed. I fell in love with you, my darling. That's why I gave myself to you so freely at the lake yesterday. That's why I want to share my future with you. That's why I asked you to come here tonight and take over. Even if you fail me in this crisis, you must remember that I love you. Do you understand that?"

I nodded.

Biz drained the glass. "Get this over in a hurry," she said crisply. "I've had enough of him in this house."

That was Biz Parente—like a chameleon. I wondered why she had not already loosed her temper on this man, and then I thought I understood that part of it. On the way to the throne room, I took my time and straightened out a number of details. Then I said to the man in the wingchair, "Mr. Crews, it's later than you realize."

He didn't stir; he was dead drunk. I rested his head on his knees and tried a method that has never yet failed me. With my hands on the sides of his neck, my thumbs massaged the tip of his spine, rotating slowly and deeply toward the brain. Within a minute he roused, and I rested his head back against the chair. When his eyes focused and he recognized me, I said, "There's something you must know."

I should have choked the life out of him because he was lower than a racketeer. This man had betrayed a public trust. Yet, he had always treated me like a gentleman and I went that way, a little longer, with him.

"Mr. Crews, I have just returned from Helldorado and the White Swan. Using his authority as sheriff, Jake Tibbs led a raiding party that smashed Helldorado. Steady Eddy Fynn, your crooked chief of detectives, is dead. Tony Scales and Pete Castille, your top lieutenants, were murdered after the raid started. All the rackets, and especially the dope-pushing, are busted wide open and all the little rats are on the lam. In Parente's garage is the county car that you use. It has a smashed front and a bullet hole in one fender. I could give you more details, but why waste time? You're finished."

He knew that. He sat there whitefaced, looking even older than his too many years. I asked, "How many persons could prove that you fat-catted this racket operation, Crews?"

He shrugged tiredly. "Not many, but numbers do not matter. I want you to listen while I explain. Believe me, Mr. Barry, as I look back, I cannot determine exactly how I arrived in this chair in this—this denouement. It seems, and you must believe this, not quite clear where and how I took the first misstep."

"Give it a try," I suggested.

"I was born in this county and raised by respectable parents who are dead now, thank God. I married into a fine family. If my wife hadn't died before the war—no, that's rationalization—she could not possibly have stopped me. I was a respectable lawyer with a fair practice. Perhaps that was the beginning—not enough money. I had a nodding acquaintance with Dominic Parente and knew he was in the rackets. He seemed rather a good sort—kind, polite, quiet, well-dressed, prosperous—and generous. This was in 1941, the first year I was president of the Red Feather drive, and it failed, as usual, to meet its quota, this time by seven thousand dollars.

"Parente came to me quietly and met the quota with cash. He insisted that the gift be anonymous. I was overwhelmed. For the first time, the county was successful in Red Feather and I was given full credit for that success. I might add that it raised me considerably in the eyes of the people. I'm still the Red Feather president. Every year there has been some deficit and every year Parente has met that deficit—with anonymous cash."

"Go on," I prodded.

"In 1943," Parente asked me to execute several deeds and tax searches. It was perfectly legitimate and I did the jobs. He paid me twice the ordinary fees. I needed his business and his cash badly. Later that same year, I reorganized one corporation for him and initiated, under his direction, three new holding companies. All this was legal, and again, Parente was overly generous. I had the best law practice I had ever enjoyed, and I was pleased.

"Let's look at his illegal operations. He controlled every racket in the county, and there was no public outcry against his operations. There were several wire rooms, so I understood, one gambling club, possibly a floating crap game, and numbers. Also, call girls, but no cheap houses and no marijuana. Only the usual things.

"Naturally, Parente had a dominant voice in county politics and controlled Ben Fairclough. Ben was the nominal party leader until his death in 1948. In 1944, to keep to the time schedule, Ben came to me and said the post of county prosecutor was open and did I want it. It was the big chance I had hoped for. As prosecutor, you continue your private law practice and—ah, certain profitable cases accrue to your private practice. Thoroughly legitimate, of course, and very profitable, I might add.

"When Ben informed me the prosecutorship was 'in the works,' as he said, I had just concluded a fat job for Parente. I brought the completed folder to him. In this very room, I said that our business relations must cease immediately, that I was to be the next prosecutor. Parente said that he understood that. He paid me five thousand dollars for the work, in cash, and when I protested that the amount was too much, Parente said to consider it a bonus. Before I left, he said something that I have never been able to forget, Mr. Barry. He said, 'Frank, if any man ever looked the part of public prosecutor, you're that man.' It was one of the highest compliments that I've ever been paid.

"I served the county to the best of my ability. But I soon discovered that I worked for Parente, that he was my boss, and in—ah, certain matters, issued the directives which I carried out. The rackets prospered. Not once did Parente step out of line. No rough stuff, no murders, no brazenness. Only *legitimate* rackets. It was quite profitable for me, and I needed money because public officials are never paid enough to live on, Mr. Barry. I was able to purchase that lovely estate where you planted daffodils the other day. I remarried, and my one regret is that I was unfaithful to my new wife. I don't know how long the arrangements between Parente and myself might have continued—perhaps indefinitely—but the end began last August when Parente had a nervous breakdown and the old order changed." He seemed puzzled, but *puzzled* was a little too mild a word for his predicament.

"Mr. Barry, can you point out my first misstep?"

I had listened carefully. In my book, he was a liar. I suppose that certain parts of the rotten story were true, but I didn't swallow his obvious rationalizations, nor the crap that certain rackets are legitimate, nor the junk about Dominic Parente being such a kind, decent, generous citizen. No racket boss ever rose to his kind of countywide, dictatorial power without leaving in his wake busted heads and broken lives, and corrupted police and grafting politicians. Every racket boss is one hundred per cent outside the law, and every racket boss is a calculating, vicious, amoral rat!

That's why I asked, "Tell me specifically how you had to take Parente's orders once you became prosecutor."

"You see, I trusted Parente," said Crews. "Two weeks after I was sworn in as prosecutor, I received a photograph through the mails. It had been snapped in this room. It showed Parente paying me five thousand dollars. The photograph was so clear in detail that you could see the denomination of several of the bills. Not once did Parente ever mention that photograph to me. I was trapped, Mr. Barry."

That's the touch of the racket boss—the soft gloved hand extended to the unwise, to the indiscreet, and frankly in this case, to the greedy. Always under the glove is the tough fist, with the sap and the gun handy, and the threats of blackmail and extortion. And always, behind all this, is the sick, smart, callous mind. That's how the unwise and the indiscreet are trapped. I felt no sympathy for this greedy, stupid fool, but he was no murderer.

"Crews, you've omitted one point. Rackets can't exist without a tough boss. After the Parente exit, somebody added dope to the rackets. Somebody opened Helldorado. You?"

He rose right up off the chair. "I shan't tell you and—"

Biz Parente didn't trust anybody. But I think Frank Crews was so ensnared by her that he would have taken the stand and testified that *he* had added dope and opened the Helldorado. She stepped into the room, her face livid with anger.

"I've taken enough crap from you!" she screamed.

She carried that heavy Luger as if it were a toy, and nobody had had to tell her it was a Luger or how to use it.

The Luger roared once. The bullet slammed into Frank Crews's chest and knocked him into the chair. When the bullet from a Luger knocks a man down, the only person who can help him is the mortician.

She turned those blazing eyes and that savage face and that smoking Luger on me. "I knew damn well you wouldn't do the job on him that had to be done! All right, he's dead! He won't bother me any longer!" And she proved to be a true chameleon. With her empire in ruins about her, she smiled. The loveliness of her face belied the evil in her heart.

"My darling, we're rid of him. Now, we can have everything together. We can go off together. Because I love you. You love me, don't you?"

"You must control your emotions by jerking on strings," I said. "Frank Crews didn't mastermind any rackets and bring dope into this county when your husband dropped from the scene. But you did."

"Don't ever say that, my darling!"

"Frank Crews couldn't mastermind a day nursery, and you know it. But *you* could, and you knew how to keep lecherous old Frank in line. For three hours I've been right behind you. Wherever you were, you left a trail. In Tony's ashtray back at Helldorado there are a handful of your half-smoked Tareytons, smeared with crimson lipstick that any amateur could match up in the laboratory. You must have worn slacks earlier, and Tony's hat. That was a smart move, but it didn't protect you for long because I'd have come here after you tonight whether we had a date or not. The trail led here, and it had to be you. Parente wouldn't have gunned his lieutenants because that's not in the gangster code. You would because you haven't got a code. When Frank Crews proved to be the fat cat, that was your finish. He's no murderer, bad as he is. You've tried to make me think you had nothing to do with the rackets, posing as the *good* housewife. But you're not home free, you amoral bitch."

"Please, my darling!"

"The trouble with you is that your judgment's bad. Why, you just shot Frank Crews and lost your best chance to go free! Why? The damn fool would have gone on the stand and exonerated you, implicating himself to play a hero's role in your eyes. How stupid can you get?"

She didn't believe me. I snapped, "Why the hell don't you shoot me with the Luger and close the last pair of lips that can convict you?"

"Darling, what about our strong love?" she murmured.

"As the boys who chase after dames say, to me you're nothing but a cheap floozy."

Any other woman would have fired the Luger, and I'd have catapulted to the floor. Not Biz Parente. She was still figuring. She exercised a strong hand on her temper, and that's more than can be said for most vicious-tempered women. They shoot first and figure the angles afterward. She had a better idea than killing me with my own gun.

"Don't move," she ordered, and backed against a divan by one wall. Next she did exactly what I wanted her to do. She kept the Luger on me and dipped one hand under the cushions. She produced a second gun in her left hand.

"So that's where you hid the .32 you used to knock off Tony and Pete," I jeered.

"It's Frank's gun, you dope. I knew better than to shoot you with your own gun. Frank came in here early tonight with this gun and—" She smiled. "I was too smart for him and got him stupid drunk. When I went to Helldorado before the raid, I didn't know there was going to be a raid, but I had Frank's gun and used it. Oh, you were clever with that raid, my darling! But not as clever as I'm going to be. I have a way out. This is the way it's going to be, you double-crossing sonuvabitch. Frank's gun killed Tony and Pete. Your gun killed Frank. Coincidentally, his gun will kill you. Clever, eh? You and Frank tried to kill each other simultaneously and you killed each other. Killing you will be a pleasure. I'm going to walk out of here free—and with the cash, big boy!"

It was time to shoot.

She tossed the Luger toward my feet, and with the skilled precision of an expert gunman, started to switch the .32 to her right hand. That's the weakness of improvisation—it wastes motion.

I had had time to think while listening to Crews's autobiography. I had anticipated the moves she had to make, and I knew how I would elude her. The split second she tossed the Luger, I dipped a hand into the pocket of my jacket and drew the .25 automatic with its safety off. When she was in the middle of the switch, I fired one shot from the waist. The bullet ripped through that white sweater exactly between those beautiful proud breasts. She pitched forward and died without a sound.

That's the beauty of this gun—it's designed for close work. It's light and fast and deadly. The trick is to believe in your marksmanship, and I was a believer.

Carrying the Garand, Willy barged into the room, late as usual. I said calmly, "We made one mistake. It wasn't Jake Tibbs. He must have gone off on some goose chase of his own. Phone Helldorado and get Jake over here in a hurry."

"She was the one we were trailing, huh?"

"It had to be Jake or her, and it was her. Run along."

I laid the .25 on a table and left everything exactly as it was. I lit a cigarette. The climax had come and I had had to kill her— that was the only way she could be stopped. With her dope racket, where the big money lay, she had ruined too many innocent lives, like poor Sherry Dalgren's, and she had to pay with her life for that. When I tumbled to the fact that Biz was behind the dope, I had known that I would have to kill her. No jury of men could convict that lovely face and that superb figure.

I was through the cigarette when Willy returned. "Jake's comin' right over with the siren wide, pal. I phoned Wanda, too"

"What did Wanda say?"

"She's glad it's over. She said somethin' about poor Ruth."

I left the room and passed through the circular lobby with its yellow globe. The telephone waited on the side table in the dim, silent hallway with the high ceiling. I sat at the table, got the operator, and said a number. Persistent ringing at the other end of the line finally produced a sleepy-voiced answer.

"Mr. Dalgren," I said, "this is the Committee of One reporting. I'll tell you some of it and you can read the rest in the papers tomorrow." I talked for one minute. "My fee? Mail it to New York. There's no hurry."

I hung up and went back to wait for Jake Tibbs.

CHAPTER THIRTEEN

O UTSIDE the bungalow on this bright morning, the first of
May, a horn tooted twice, and I said, "Let's get it over with
kids."

Wanda was breathless and dewy-eyed but a trifle wan. She
wore an off-the-face blue hat, a blue tailored suit, white gloves,
and high-heeled black pumps. Willy was downright uncomfort-
able in his Sunday suit, his necktie awry although I had reknot-
ted it a moment previously. They had taken out their marriage
license, passed their Wassermann test, and let three days elapse,
as required by New Jersey law. I was the best man. Waiting in the
convertible was Ruth Crews, the matron of honor.

Wanda walked over to Willy. She grasped the lapels of his
coat and worried the cloth. Willy said, "What's the matter, kid?"

"Willy, ever since—well, I've *tried* and *tried* to tell you before,
but you wouldn't listen! Before it's too late, you've *got* to listen!
I—I can't keep this from you! That morning I walked up to your
stand—I mean, I *must* tell you where I had been and what I had
been doing! Willy, I was—"

Willy clamped a huge paw over her mouth. "Shut up, see?
You love me, huh?"

I stared out the kitchen window and glimpsed a row of daffodils marching in golden silence through the bright sunlight,
and then those cathedral bells began to peal again.

"Willy, I love you! Only you, Willy! You're my god!"

Willy said, "That's all I want to hear, kid. Run out to Ruth before she has a fit."

The screen door slammed and high heels clacked. That's my pal, Willy Pickle. Just a big, genial, simple lug, with no more brains in his head than a—

"You know," Willy said thoughtfully, "I ain't worried about her past and I ain't worried about our future, either. I lied to you when you come here that first night, pal. I knew her name was Wanda Spurling, but I didn't tell you that because you might have got the wrong idea about that kid, her bein' an ex-call girl, see?" The horn tooted imperiously. "Me, I'm gettin' scared. You go out first, see? You're the best man, pal."

I didn't go out first. I pushed Willy ahead of me. In my book, Willy was the best man.

THE END